Flexin' On My Ex, Loving A Boss

T. MICHELLE

Copyright

Copyright © 2024 by T. Michelle

All rights reserved. No part of this book may be reproduced in any form or by any electronic or mechanical means, including information storage and retrieval systems, without written permission from the author, except for the use of brief quotations in a book review.

This novel is a work of fiction. Any resemblances to actual events, real people, living or dead, organizations, establishments or locales are products of the author's imagination. Other names, characters, places, and incidents are used fictitiously.

Synopsis

De'arra Kingston finds herself at a breaking point in her long-term relationship with Izzy after stepping up to cover the relationship's slack. Unexpectedly, Izzy offers her as collateral to settle a $100,000 debt. Now, she must spend three weeks with a complete stranger, but what if this man turns out to be a charming, irresistibly good-looking guy with a substantial bank balance?

Assad Lattimore is a money-focused man who's been burned by women, including his ex-girlfriend's public rejection of his proposal. With a thriving record label and his protégé brother, Trevin, by his side, Assad is financially successful but missing one key element in his life – a woman.

Paige Kingston escapes an abusive relationship and discovers what a good man is when she meets Trevin Lattimore. Auditioning for a movie produced by the Lattimore brothers, she lands the lead role alongside Trevin, leading to a sizzling connection. Even Trevin's obsessive ex couldn't extinguish the sparks flying between them.

Discover the twists and turns in "Flexin' On My Ex, Loving A Boss" as these characters navigate complex relationships and find unexpected love.

Catalog

A Corporate Thug Captured My Heart 1-3
Wife Of A Corporate Thug: What Happens In Vegas Stays In Vegas (Spin-Off)
Finessing The Heart Of A Player: From The Hood To A Mansion 1-3
Loyal To A Coldblooded Hoodlum: Bazar And Paradise 1-3

Chapter One

DE'ARRA

"Whew! I don't even want to see the salon or hear the words crimp, wand curls, lace front, or any of that shit for the next three weeks," I said to myself as I burst into my apartment and kicked off my custom-made periwinkle blue crocs with my name painted on them. My dogs were doing more than barking. Those muthafuckas were howling even though there wasn't a moon in sight.

"Hey, babe." I greeted my longtime boyfriend, Ishmael, who was sitting at the kitchen table, rolling up as usual. I kept telling his ass he was going to turn into a damn blunt as much as he smoked. I hated the smell and the fact that he acted like he couldn't live without it, but because I loved his ass, I put up with it.

Throwing my things down onto the couch, I made my way over to him. We'd gotten into an argument this morning before I left about him helping out more with the bills, groceries, and just shit around the crib that I felt I shouldn't be doing. Izzy didn't have a real job like me, but he made a little money here and there gambling, selling weed, and shit like that. According to him, he wasn't made for a nine-to-five lifestyle, which was cool and everything, but if I was going to be the breadwinner until he 'figured out his life,' then he needed to do better as my man—no, scratch that—as a man in general.

"What's good, beautiful?"

I wrapped my arms around his neck, and he leaned in to kiss me after wrapping his big, strong arms around me.

"You smell good." I caught a whiff of him just as we pulled away from our hug and smiled, pecking his lips once more.

"Damn, get up off me with your thirsty ass. Don't make me get my other girl to beat you up," he joked, causing me to smirk and mush his head.

"If you wanna send that hoe, whoever she is, to the ICU, then be my guest."

He chuckled, lifting his blunt to his lips and lighting it.

"I'll tell her she better tread fucking lightly then." He pulled from his blunt, never losing eye contact with me.

"Mhm, she better." I immediately tried to back away since I knew he was going to blow the smoke in my direction.

This fool held onto me, pulling me even closer than I already was, and blew the smoke in my face. I quickly punched him in the arm with all my might, causing him to let me go.

"Ahh. Damn, baby, I was just fucking with you."

"That's what you get. You play too damn much." He rotated his arm in a circle, trying to ease the pain as I walked into the kitchen. "Chinese food again? Really?" I quizzed more so to myself than to Izzy.

He sucked his teeth as I looked at him over the kitchen island. "Is that a problem?"

"No, Izzy, it's not a problem." I spun around, mumbling about his ass, and retrieved a pitcher of cherry Kool-Aid to go with the Chinese food that was apparently dinner for the night.

"Don't mumble under your breath, De'arra. Please, by all means, speak up."

I pointed at him like I was scolding a damn child, but I didn't care because he was irking my nerves, and I hadn't even been home long. "I'm not doing this with you again today, Ishmael." I went to the pantry to grab a paper plate, only to discover there weren't any. "So, you couldn't go pick up more plates?"

This was a constant thing between us. We could laugh and play, but two seconds later, we were at each other's throats. I hated it.

"Man, I was busy, and you know that. Plus, it slipped my mind, so chill out. It ain't that deep. Just use a real plate out of the cabinet or a bowl."

Slamming the door to the pantry, I sped out of the kitchen and scooped up my shit from the couch.

"Whatchu you doing? You not gon' eat?"

"Boy, fuck you!"

I headed for the bedroom, having lost my appetite. I didn't know how the hell I was going to get through the next three weeks with him behaving like that. I had taken a much-needed vacation from work but saw that this was going to be a problem and we'd probably end up killing each other. I had a few online classes that I was almost done with, and my grades were slipping, so the time I took off would be spent catching up on schoolwork but more so to get a woosah from my entitled ass clients.

He hopped up and was right on my trail.

"What, Izzy?" I spat as he pulled my arm.

"Wait, baby... chill. I'm sorry. I just got a lot of shit on my mind, and I just..." He sighed, peering down into my furious and now semi-wet eyes.

"What could possibly be on your mind, Izzy? I pay the bills in this bitch! I cook, I clean, take out the trash, and whatever else you could think of around this muthafucka. You leave here every day and go post up on a fucking block, Izzy. Then you come home after doing the bare minimum, put a lil hundred dollars on the table, maybe even two hundred, and think shit is all good! News flash! Rent is fourteen hundred dollars, and they're trying to go up on it, so excuse me for not understanding why you would even have the audacity to fix your mouth to tell me you're stressed!"

Rubbing his hand down his face, he had the nerve to look annoyed. Hell, I would be annoyed, too, if my girlfriend, who I claimed to love, had to give me the same speech practically every day over some shit I should've been doing as a man. I was so damn glad that this shit was all in my name and that I had a little saved for a rainy day. I knew I shouldn't have been complaining since I could easily find myself another man with my fine ass, but I wanted this one to get his shit together.

Being brown-skinned, five foot three, fun size with a handful of booty and just enough titties was enough to have all these niggas at my feet. Well, at least that's what men told me, as their envious ass girlfriends and bad body baby mamas stalked me, threatened me, and tried to fight me.

With a '90s styled tapered haircut, succulent lips juicer than a steak, thick thighs, and chinked light brown eyes that smiled at you and twinkled when in the sun, I was a sight to see. The Marilyn Monroe mole above my lip on my left side really set my look off, along with my pierced nose and lip piercing smack dab in the middle of my bottom lip. I worked out a lot when I wasn't slaying hair at my sister Paige's shop.

Paige was older than me by two years, but you'd never be able to tell since I was more like her little big sister. I always had to bail her out of some type of situation, especially with her no good ass boyfriend, Millz. He stayed putting his hands on her and blackening her beautiful face, but she had yet to leave him because she was dickmatized. That's all it could be because it wasn't like he was any better than Ishmael. He was in the streets also. In fact, they were the best of buds. Everyone wanted the Kingston sisters, but we just had to give up the box to these two lame ass niggas. The shit was crazy if you asked me.

"Don't talk to me like that, De'arra. I hate when you do that. I wasn't trying to argue with you, and I apologized. The fuck you just go off on me for? If you don't wanna be with me, then fucking don't! A nigga ain't twisting your arm or putting a gun to your head, so why stay?" he yelled, towering over me at six foot one. "Tell me. Why in the fuck are you with me?"

I wiped the tears that had fallen from my eyes and pushed him back. "I love you. That's why! Shit didn't always used to be like this between us. You showed me a different side of you when we first got together four years ago, but now..." I sniffled, wiping more tears that wouldn't stop falling. "Now, you're deep in the streets. You come home late all the time, we don't go out anymore, we barely have sex, and... you don't help me with shit."

"Baby, listen to me." Izzy grabbed the items in my arms and laid them back on the couch. He then took my hands into his. "I'm sorry I made you feel this way, and I promise things will change. Just don't leave me. A nigga really loves you for real, and you know that."

"No, I don't know that, Izzy. Or else, I wouldn't feel this way."

He kissed the back of my hands. "Things will be different; you have my word on that shit, but... I do have to tell you something."

Snatching my hands away, with balled-up lips, I shifted all my weight to one side. "What? I swear to God that if you've been trickin' off on me, I'm sending you to meet him."

"What?" He sucked his teeth. "Nah, baby, I ain't trickin' off."

Placing my hand over my forehead, all I could do was glare at him because I felt like he was about to say something crazy.

"Then what? Huh?"

Licking his lips, he got really silent, further pissing me off and raising my damn blood pressure. His lips parted a few times as if he were trying to gather his words, yet he still said nothing.

"Goodnight, Izzy."

I didn't even get a chance to turn around before he blurted out, "I'm in debt with a nigga by the name of Assad Lattimore."

My brows rose, confused about why he was even telling me this. "Okay, so pay that nigga. Why are you acting all weird about it? You know what you need to do and—"

"I owe him a lot, and this nigga ain't nothing to play with. I've been hustling and trying to get the money up, but that nigga said my time was up, and I'd be in a body bag come Monday if I... if I didn't get him the money ASAP."

"What's a lot, Izzy? What are we talking?"

"It's uh... one hundred thousand."

I opened my mouth to speak, but nothing came out. I was beyond shocked by the number he said.

"W-what in the hell have you really been out here doing to owe someone so much money?" I realized after he didn't say anything that I probably didn't want to know the answer to that question. "You know what? I don't even want to know, but I hope you have a plan because—"

Izzy cut me off again. "Instead of the money back, all he's asking is for you to spend three weeks with him. I swear, baby, this was not my idea. He saw a picture of you on my lock screen and then—"

"Wait, what? Are you fucking crazy? You think you can just go around offering my pussy to a random nigga because you owe him money?" He had to be losing his mind because there was no way in hell he should have thought this shit was okay.

I couldn't bite my tongue on this one. He'd gotten us into some crazy ass situations over the course of our relationship, but this shit took the cake. Out of all the things Izzy could have done, he chose to pimp me out—his girlfriend whom he claimed to love so much.

"Baby, I didn't offer. He..." he started to say, but I put up my hand, instantly silencing him as he dropped his head in shame.

"Don't baby me, Ishmael! My pussy barely belongs to you, and now you think you're about to pimp me out, all because you can't pay your debt?" I crossed my arms across my breasts as my chest rose and fell.

He quickly looked up, sucking his teeth in the process. "Fuck you mean by that?"

He had to be smoking on some shit other than weed because everything I'd just said was more than easy to comprehend.

"I mean just that, Izzy! I have not been happy in this relationship for a while now, and you know that." I stepped closer to him, getting into his personal space. He looked at me angrily as if I were the one in the wrong. "Despite all the shit we've been through, I loved your ass through it all, and this is the shit you do?"

"Bae... it's just sex."

Had he not been taller than me and had the body of a linebacker, I would have slapped the taste clean out of his mouth.

Izzy was brown-skinned with a fade, thicker than I normally liked my men, but he wasn't sloppy with the shit. He was hard body with light brown eyes and plump lips, which were surprisingly not dark, even after all the smoking he did. Although he dressed nicely, it was nothing too fancy since the nigga was broke. He was tatted up, mainly on his arms, neck, and chest, had a massive beard, straight ass teeth, courtesy of having braces as a child. Izzy gave me Money Bagg Yo vibes, always smelled good, had a decent-sized dick, enough to ride, and was still one of the finest niggas I had ever been with. But right now, he looked like an infection between a bitch's toes!

"Okay, so you fuck him, then! Yeah, settle your own debt, and you fuck him!"

"Yo, chill out with that gay shit!" His deep voice echoed through the apartment.

It was now time for me to raise my voice another octave. "No, you chill! This shit is not okay!"

I pushed his firm chest as hard as I could. He tried to latch onto my wrist, but I snatched away.

"Do not touch me!" I warned. "Of all the people to offer up, why didn't you offer your cracked out ass mama? Everyone knows she'll fuck whoever, whenever, and however for a fix!"

I watched as he gritted his teeth, staring at me through the slits of his eyes. I'd certainly hit a soft spot with that one, but I didn't give a damn. I wanted his ass to hurt the same way I was. It didn't feel good to know that I basically meant nothing to him.

"Take that shit back right now, De'arra! You don't really mean that!"

Cocking my head to the side, I was taken aback by his words. "Oh, I don't?" I chuckled, infuriating him further. "I meant every word, so I won't be taking anything back! At least she willingly gives her pussy to niggas."

With that, I turned to walk away, rolling my eyes in the process. I didn't care to finish the conversation. I was tired, needed a hot shower, and didn't want to hear him utter another word for the rest of the night.

Chapter Two

PAIGE

"Assad fucking Lattimore?" I shouted as I relaxed in a nice, warm bubble bath. "You have to be kidding right now, DeDe."

"What?"

My sister called me in a panic. I didn't know what the fuck happened since she was speaking so fast and crying all in the phone. Once I finally got her to calm down, she told me that her boyfriend, Izzy, had pretty much offered her pussy up on a platter to one of the finest and richest niggas on the planet right now.

"Bitch, not only is the man fine as hell but he is paid! He owns *Keep It Real* records, and his label birthed some of the hottest rappers in Atlanta. No, scratch that. His label birthed some of the hottest rappers in the game right now, including his fine ass younger brother, Trevin Lattimore, but his rap name is Tre Bang.

"Okay, and?" She didn't understand what I was getting at.

I sighed. "Sis, I swear you live under a rock. My point is that you're always complaining about the things that Izzy doesn't do. Well, you're going to get a chance to be Assad Lattimore's girl, his hoe, or whatever it is that he wants you to be for three whole weeks! Bitch, you better milk that fucking cow!"

If I was her, I wouldn't even mind fucking on his rich ass. By the end of those three weeks, his accounts would be drier than a bitch's hair with heat damage.

"Okay." She sniffled. "Well, you fuck him then. I'm not even the least bit interested in any of this. I just wanted to enjoy my time off, get a little self-care done, catch up on my schoolwork, maybe read a book, visit some new restaurants, and lay up with my man. But now he can kiss my natural black ass." She began to cry once more.

"Aww, sis, don't cry. You know I was just being funny to lighten the mood. At the end of the day, it's your body, and you don't have to pay off Izzy's debt with it. He got himself into that shit, and it's not your fault or obligation to save his ass."

"Thank you." She blew her nose, causing me to shake my head.

"Of course, sis, you know I love you, and I'm always going to be on your side. Izzy is real fucked up for this shit, and just know I'm with you on whatever you decide. If you wanna leave him, bitch, I'll help you pack his shit. But... if you wanna see what it's like being on the arm of a rich nigga for three weeks, I won't judge you."

"I honestly don't know what to do. Izzy said that this Assad guy is dangerous and not to be fucked with. I don't want to come home one day, and Izzy's head is decapitated and sitting in the middle of my table. As much as I hate him right now, I don't want him dead." De'arra blew her nose again.

"Nah, trust me, I feel you on that. It's easier said than done. Honestly, I wouldn't know what to do if I were in your shoes, DeDe. You've been with Izzy for four years, and you know nothing about Assad. For all we know, he could be a man by day and a vampire by night, sucking bitches' blood and shit."

De'arra burst out laughing. "Bitch, shut up. You just be saying shit, and only you can make me burst out laughing while I'm in the middle of crying."

I heard a loud noise coming from the bedroom, which caused me to quickly sit up and some of the water in the tub to spill onto the floor.

"Listen, you know I watch a lot of movies, but that shit could happen for real." I pulled the plug at the bottom of the tub to drain it as I stood. "Let me call you back, though."

"Aight. Please make sure you do. I'm distraught."

I couldn't help but laugh at my little sis. "Girl, go shower and lay your distraught ass down. I think Millz is home, so let me go tend to his ass."

De'arra scoffed, and I was almost certain she was probably rolling her eyes at that very moment. "Okay. He better not be on no shit because I don't mind hopping in my car tonight."

She was referring to Millz's abuse, which we were both very familiar with since we were very close, and I always called her when things got too bad. I always tried to fight back, but that always made shit worse.

I damn near wet up the whole floor as I hopped out of the tub and placed my towel around my waist. Snatching the bathroom door open, I saw exactly what I expected to see. Millz was pissy drunk, stumbling all around the room, bumping into everything as he attempted to remove his clothes. I rolled my eyes at the sight of him.

"B-Bae." His words slurred, and I couldn't do shit but roll my eyes again. I was sick of this same song and dance with him. He just couldn't do right, and I was tired of complaining about it. I could have any nigga I wanted, trust and believe, but I wanted him to do right for me… for us. I deserved it, and after putting in so much time with him, a bitch was comfortable and not trying to start over with the next nigga, that's for sure.

"Bring yo' fine ass here." He stumbled over to me and wrapped his arm around my neck. I tried to walk him over to the bed, but he was too busy trying to kiss all over my face.

"Babe, stop! You're drunk," I spat.

A few moments later, after practically dragging his heavy ass body across the room, I shoved him down onto the bed. This fool started laughing for whatever reason, but I ignored it as I got on my knees to remove his shoes and socks.

Millz wasn't small, but he wasn't big either. He was kind of in the middle. He was inked up, had brown skin, curly hair with tapered sides, dark brown eyes, and gave me Diggy Simmons vibes but finer. We weren't aways on bad terms, but when he started hitting me, it seemed that he never stopped, and our relationship was never really the same. I tried my hardest to fix whatever I was doing that was pissing him off, but to no avail. When he didn't make as much money on the block, he was pissed. When he gambled and lost a lot of money, he was pissed. Every little thing ticked him off. He was nothing like the man I fell for, yet I stayed, hoping he'd shed this horrible persona and become the man I couldn't live without again.

I was too damn fine for this shit. One thing about it and two things for sure, I wasn't cocky; I just knew for a fact that everything about me screamed bad bitch. My little sister was brown-skinned, while I was a little lighter. I considered myself to have a butter pecan skin tone. Taking after our mother, I had long, curly hair that reached the middle of my back, but I often wore it straight. It was jet black. My eyes were a pretty amber color, and I had deep dimples in my cheeks and back dimples that all the niggas used to love before Maynard, also known as Millz, snatched me up.

I had a nice, jiggly home-grown ass, hourglass physique, and a lil' stomach, but nothing a few sit-ups couldn't cure. I didn't have any piercings other than my ears, and I didn't have any tattoos either. Standing at about five foot seven, I was definitely a head-turner, which is why it baffled me every day that I looked in the mirror and saw the bruises Millz left on me, knowing I could do better.

Part of me stayed with him because I was simply comfortable. He was all I had known for the past few years, and I didn't want to start over with someone else. I knew it was a stupid reason for staying, yet there I was. I was afraid that I could possibly move on with someone else and things would be worse than they currently were with Millz and me. What if I simply couldn't find better?

"Come ride this dick, baby."

I scoffed because he had been gone all day, wasn't responding to my calls or text messages, and then had the nerve to come home and interrupt my relaxing bath time with this mess. Plus, he'd just gone upside my head last night after promising he wouldn't put his hands on me again, so we weren't exactly on the best of terms.

I stood to finish helping him undress. "Boy, no. This black eye says I shouldn't even be tending to you right now, but I'm a good, loyal woman, so you're lucky I'm even doing this. Now, sit up."

I had to help him sit up so I could remove his shirt. Just as I was about to question him about where he'd been, someone started banging on the front door. Our spot wasn't too big, so I could definitely hear it loud and clear.

"The fuck?" I said to myself as I rushed off to see who was banging like they lost their mind.

I looked through the peephole and couldn't believe who it was.

"Marjorie, what in the hell are you doing here, and so late at that, banging on my door?"

Marjorie was the mother of Millz's three-year-old son. He was a cutie pie, and I loved Marion to pieces, but his mama was a piece of work. I disliked her because she disliked me. It was simple. Sis had an issue with me getting with Millz from the get-go. According to her, he was just going through a phase after their breakup, and getting with me was just going to be some rebound type shit.

He and I had been together for two and a half years, so obviously, this was more than a rebound type of situation. In the beginning, she was always interfering with our relationship by calling about things not pertaining to their son, popping up, and just doing the most. As time went by, things calmed down. She got her own man, according to Millz, and she pretty much left us alone. That's why I was surprised to see her tonight because she hadn't popped up over there in ages.

She looked as if she had seen a ghost. "Wait. W-what are you doing here?"

"Bitch... are you okay? You ain't smoking that stuff, is you?"

I didn't understand why she was there and questioning me about me being at my own crib.

"You and Millz got back together?"

My brows rose at her odd question. "We never broke up. What are you talking about? And you still haven't answered my question about why you're banging on the door."

"I uh... I was trying to reach Millz, but it's cool. I'll just go."

She rubbed her belly, which I could see was protruding, and took off fast as hell. That shit was weird as hell, and I felt like something was up. I slammed the door and marched back into our bedroom, ready to question Millz about Marjorie popping up and asking if we broke up, but he was snoring loud as shit. Whenever he got like that, it was no use trying to wake him from anything, so I reached into his pants pocket in search of his phone.

My heart was beating overtime as I typed in his code. Sure enough, he hadn't changed it, so I went straight to his thread with Marjorie. To my surprise, she sent him a message as I was holding the phone, causing it to chime. Looking over at him, I eyed his movements while placing his phone on silent.

Marjorie

Umm, I'm confused as hell on why Paige is there. You told me the two of you had broken up, and she moved out, which is the only reason I got back involved with you. It all makes sense now as to why you never wanted me to chill at your spot. I feel so damn stupid for getting pregnant again by your no-good ass.

Pregnant? Again? Did this bitch just say she was pregnant by my man again?

Something came over me because I felt like I was having an out-of-body experience or some shit as I threw the cellphone at him with all my might. It hit him in the face, just like ol' girl who got hit in the face on stage by a cell phone.

"Ahh!" he roared, shooting up from his slumber, holding his face. "Paige, what the fuck are you doing?"

"You got Marjorie pregnant again? Huh?"

He climbed off the bed, still holding his face, but I didn't give a damn. I ran toward him and started giving his ass the business as he yelled for me to stop.

"Chill, bruh! The fuck is you on?"

I kept hitting him anywhere I could but instantly stopped when he backhanded me with all his might, sending me to the floor with a loud thud.

He hit me so hard that I was in a daze. I tried my best to look up at him, but the whole room was spinning.

"Baby… I'm sorry. I didn't mean to do that. It's just that you were swinging on me and… I'm sorry."

Millz tried to help me up, but I pushed his hands away.

"Y-you need to pack your shit and g-get the hell out!" I was out of breath as I struggled to stand, now also holding my stinging face. "Take your phone with you and go. Hell, I don't care where you go, but you can't stay here."

I grabbed my phone and ran into the bathroom, then quickly locked the door behind me.

I couldn't do shit but slide down the door like I was in a music video and cry my eyes out as Millz tried to jiggle the handle and apologize.

Chapter Three

DE'ARRA

"You sleep?" Izzy asked as I lay on my side, wide awake, staring at the wall. He leaned closer to me, I guess trying to see if he could tell if I was awake.

I sighed. "No, Izzy, but I damn sure don't wanna talk to you, so please... just stop."

"Look." He placed his hand on my shoulder, pulling me to face him. "I know what I did was fucked up, but I swear on everything I love that if you do this one thing for me, I will get my shit together. I wanna make you smile more and make you actually happy to see a nigga come through the door."

"Yes, the shit is wrong, but I decided that I'll do it. I do love you, but you know that. I want us to figure things out to better our relationship, but I won't be able to do that if you're dead." I chuckled as he reached for my hand, bringing it to his lips.

"Thank you," he mumbled with his lips against my hand. "I owe you big time for this and—"

My phone began to ring, startling me since it was damn near two in the morning. Izzy looked at me crazy, but I already knew who was calling since I didn't talk to anyone but my damn sister.

Picking up the phone, I confirmed that it was, in fact, her when I saw her name on the caller ID.

"Hey, sis. Whatever it is, can it wait until morning? I'm tired as hell and—"

"He hit me again, and he..." Sniffling and sobbing loudly into the phone, Paige said, "His baby mama is pregnant again by him. Honestly, De'arra, my heart can't take any more of this. It's literally broken, and there's nothing he can say to make me stay with him this time. I'm so hurt."

I quickly sat up in bed. "Okay, uh... just let me get some clothes on, and then I'll be over there."

"Okay," she replied, still crying her eyes out.

I felt so bad because I could hear the pain in her voice. This shit felt different than all the other times she called me crying over Millz. The nerve of him to get his baby mama pregnant again.

Niggas ain't shit.

"What? What's wrong?" Izzy asked.

I ignored him as I ran to the closet and stripped out of my night clothes.

"Is he still there?"

"Honestly, I don't know. I locked myself in the bathroom."

"Okay. Stay in there, and don't come out."

Izzy hopped out of bed and walked over to the closest to where I was slipping a shirt over the leggings I had already put on.

"Baby, tell me what's going on," he demanded.

I sucked my teeth. "Girl, hold on." Looking up at Izzy, I said, "Listen, you already know what the fuck is going on. It's the same shit that always happens. Your homeboy put his hands on my sister, and you know I don't play that. I'm about to go stomp a hole in his ass, so you might want to go ahead and warn him."

"I already told your ass to stay out of their business. It's not that fucking hard and—"

My head instantly jerked to the side. "See, that's what we not gon' do! You're barely out of the doghouse, so you have no room to talk about what's going on. Regardless, she is my sister, so I'm going to be there for her no matter what. You can take the side of that idiot if you want to, but I'm not! I don't fuck around when it comes to my blood!"

He just stood there, looking stupid as hell, as I slipped my shoes on. "Hey, my bad about that. I'm on my way," I quickly said into the receiver before ending the call.

I grabbed my keys from the nightstand, grabbed my purse, and started power walking out of the room. I locked the door and began the long ass journey to my car. Our apartment complex barely had any parking, so I had parked a whole building over from ours.

My thighs were burning by the time I got to my car, and just as I was about to hop in, Izzy jogged up to me. I didn't even realize his ass was behind me.

This nigga is getting on my nerves.

"Yes?" I threw all my shit inside. "Is there a reason you followed me? I'm in a rush."

"Look, I'm sorry about all of this, and I'm sorry for trying to interfere with you and your sister."

"Really, Izzy? I already said I'll help you with your stupid debt. You don't have to lay it on so thick right now and be all extra nice when you know you're team Millz."

"What?" He screwed up his face, looking stupid yet again. "I'm not trying to lay anything on thick, bae. I'm being dead ass serious."

"Okay." I sighed. "I just don't have time for this, so I'll see you when I get... or actually, scratch that. I'll probably stay over at Paige's, so I'll see you in the morning."

"Okay, but it's one last thing I need to tell you."

"What, Izzy? Damn! You're just full of a bunch of fucking surprises tonight, huh?"

Bitch, you already knew he followed you out here for a reason, so don't act surprised.

"Well, Assad wants to meet with us... well, you, tomorrow." He looked away from me, probably feeling like less of a man for this shit. Or at least that's how I hoped he felt. "He doesn't uh... he doesn't want me to be there, but I would feel more comfortable if someone is there with you. I know Paige is going through it tonight, but do me a favor and check with her once she's in her right mind and see if she'll go with you."

I simply nodded, ready to dead the conversation as he pulled me into him for a hug. For some reason, this hug felt different. I couldn't quite put my finger on it, though.

Izzy tried to kiss me, but I turned my face because I wasn't in a kissing type of mood.

"I love you," he said as I finally hopped in the car.

"I love you too."

Closing my driver-side door, I threw on my AC due to the bi-polar ass weather in Atlanta, cranked my car, and peeled out of there like a bat out of hell.

A bat out of hell, bitch? What does that even mean for real?

* * *

"Bitch!" Millz shouted when I slapped fire from his ass.

I was happy to see his car still outside, so I used my key to get into my sister's house. What I wasn't expecting was to see him lying out on the couch, sleeping peacefully after he'd just terrorized my damn sister, and she'd just found out that he got his baby mama pregnant again. I was so sick and tired of this man always doing wrong and putting his hands on her, so I was about to put my hands on him. Although I was small, I had a powerful ass punch ready and waiting for his ass.

He must've thought I was Paige, so he hopped up, ready to fight, until I slapped him again, knocking the sleep straight off his face.

"De'arra?" he asked, distraughtly stumbling all over the place.

"In the flesh, nigga!" I threw my things down and pounced on him. All I saw was red. "You wanna keep hitting on my sister? Huh? Well, hit me, motherfucker!"

He flailed his arms around, trying to get me off him and hollering for Paige to help. I was on him like white on rice and had a firm grip as I clawed at his eyes. I was two seconds from turning this nigga into Evander Holyfield Junior before Paige pulled me off him.

"De'arra, stop! You don't have to fight him. He's not even worth it."

I was breathing hard as he held onto his bleeding face. I smirked because I was happy about my handiwork.

"Bitch, you... you..." He looked at his hand and saw the blood. "I'm bleeding."

"Good! That will teach you about fucking around on my sister and making her your punching bag with your weak ass! Ughhh! I can't stand the fact that Izzy hangs out with you! I would hate for you to rub off on him because then I'm gonna have to beat his ass like I just did yours!"

"Paige... baby... get your sister!" He sounded like a straight-up bitch, and I couldn't help but snicker.

"No, you need to leave, Millz. I thought you were already gone!"

Looking back and forth between the two of us, he seemed to be at a loss for words, but he shouldn't have been because he knew what he did."

"Bae. Come on, is you serious? I don't even know what you're talking about, and you're doing all this shit for nothing. Marjorie may be pregnant again, but it damn sure ain't by me. I have nothing to do with that. I swear to god."

"I don't care. You need to either leave on your own, or I will call the police." Pointing to her face, Paige said, "I mean, it's up to you. I'm sure this huge black eye on my face won't be hard to miss."

Throwing his hands up in mock surrender, Millz left the second those words came out her mouth.

"Ugh! What a fucking loser!" I said the second the door slammed behind him.

I quickly turned to my sister and placed my hand on her shoulder. "Are you okay?"

She shook her head. "No, but I will be." She gave me a faint smile as tears fell from her eyes.

"Aww, it's okay, bookie. I know this shit hurts now, but like you said, you will be okay, and I wholeheartedly agree. You are so much better than him... than this. You're so pretty and so smart. You can have any man you want. I know I'm the pot calling the kettle black, but I'm serious. You could have a line of niggas willing and ready to treat you like the queen you are if you really wanted them to. You don't have to deal with an abusive cheater."

"I know, and I swear that this time..." She sniffled, wiping her eyes with the back of her hand. "I'm leaving him for good. I can't take any more of this."

Chapter Four

ASSAD

"Thanks for hitting me up."
Skooly, one of my long-time security guards, had informed me that my baby brother, Trevin, was at it again with his baby mama, Kim. The two of them were like oil and water, which was odd since they obviously had to like each other enough to lay down and make two kids.

Then, on top of that, they weren't even together. But since he was still fucking on her, even though I told him not to, Kim felt like there was still some hope of them getting back together. Trevin being a hot rap artist with hoes falling to his feet at every corner he turned, did nothing to help their situation. In fact, it made things worse.

This nigga was supposed to be finishing up his album at one of the most well-known studios in the city, which just happened to be owned by yours truly. I left early to simply clear my head since I had a lot on my plate with this tour I had planned for Trevin and a few of my other artists, making sure all bills were paid for our grandma, who was in a home, dealing with Trevin losing brand deals due to his temper, and so much more.

Being woken up out of my sleep to come and scold this dumb ass nigga wasn't exactly on my agenda, but hey, there I was.

"Trevin, what the fuck you got going on right now? I'm not paying you to argue with your baby mama all fucking night and—"

"Uh, I can hear you!" Kim smacked her lips, placing her hand on her hip. "Hello to you too, Assad."

She rolled her eyes, and so did I on the sly because I couldn't stand her for anything in this world. She was cool at first until my studio took off, and I signed Trevin, who, by the way, was one hell of a rapper. He didn't even write his shit down half the time. He was always spitting some fire shit straight off the dome.

Kim was a regular ass bitch who ain't never had shit. She wasn't necessarily a hood rat, but she was close enough to that shit. She and Trevin only had one kid before he got signed, and then, all of a sudden, before the ink even dried, she was coming around a lot more than usual.

When she got knocked up again, I didn't think much of it until she started threatening Trevin about putting him on child support. She always had her hand out and threatened to take his kids from him on several occasions. Then, I was sure she wasn't using that money to even help the kids since her jobless ass always kept her hair and nails done on top of rocking the hottest and latest shit. I couldn't stand that bitch, and she knew it.

Trevin, who was holding his bleeding lip, remained silent as he gave her the death glare. I looked around the studio and noticed that a few things were out of place, so they must've been in there tussling. Luckily for both of them, nothing looked broken.

"You gotta go," I said, looking Kim in the eyes so she knew I meant business and wasn't there for her shenanigans and shit.

"No, I'm not leaving. I'm not done talking to Trevin about this." Kim paused and reached into her purse. She retrieved a small gold hoop earring and held it up to my face. "Your brother has been fucking around with some groupie ass bitch, and I came here to get down to the bottom of it."

Before I could respond, one of Kim's friends, who I also couldn't stand, walked in. I gave that bitch dick one time, and she literally never got off it.

I sucked my teeth. "I don't give a damn about y'all bullshit! Argue with him outside my studio and take your hoe ass friend with you!"

Gasping as if what I said wasn't true, Myra wiped the corners of her mouth and placed her hand on her chest. "Really, Assad? A hoe? Nigga, you got me fucked up!"

Throwing down her bag in a rage, she squared up like she was ready to fight as I heard Trevin snicker behind me. I clenched my jaw and didn't even bother to look back at him. All of this was his fault anyway.

"Wait... Myra, calm down, bitch!" Kim tried to calm her down because she knew I didn't play that shit. I was cool for the most part, but once the beast was awakened, it was hard to put that motherfucker away.

"Yeah, listen to your fucking friend. You know I don't play that shit. I said get out, and I swear to God, if you make me repeat it, we gon' have some problems. You understand?"

Myra scoffed, placing her hands on her hips. "You know you can't treat people like this, right? Like, who just sleeps with someone and then throws them away like a piece of trash the next day?"

I shook my head. "You know that's not what the fuck happened. You're a groupie looking for a come-up. You offered pussy, we fucked, and that was it. You caught feelings, but whose fault is that? I know you didn't expect me to wife you up when all you do is come around and fuck on all my partnas. What? You think I didn't see you walk up in here, wiping your mouth like you just finished sucking dick?"

Myra looked shocked, as if I didn't know what went down at my studio. She was always hanging around, trying to bait these niggas, and they took it every time. I peeped her game, which was exactly why she only got the dick once.

Skooly re-entered the room. "Is everything good, boss?"

"Girl, come on. Let's just go," Kim said and grabbed Myra's arm. "He ain't even worth it, and neither is my BD." Kim rolled her eyes at Trevin, who smirked.

"No!" Myra snatched away. "Let me say one more thing first!" It was then that I noticed she had stumbled while walking closer to me, so she was more than likely intoxicated. I didn't even flinch as she got in my face. "Nigga, fuck you! I hate you!"

I nodded at Skooly, who was just waiting for me to give him the cue. He reached over and grabbed both Myra and Kim by the arm and started dragging them out while they both yelled obscenities.

The second the three of them left the room, Trevin started with his excuses. "My bad, bruh. I didn't ask her to come here. This bitch snuck and shared my location to her phone without my knowledge, so she would know where I was at all times. She started accusing me of fucking around on her, even though we're not together, and—"

I cut him off midsentence. "No cap... I don't even wanna hear shit you have to say. I'm saying this to you as your boss and as a brother at the same time. You need to focus on your music and leave Kim's dumbass alone. She ain't nothing but trouble and a gold digger at that. The fact that you even had not one but two children by her is ridiculous, but that's neither here nor there."

Trevin sucked his teeth. "Really, bruh?"

"Yes, really, nigga! Focus on the music, stop fucking around with Kim, stop fucking around with all these groupie hoes before you catch some shit, and stop fucking up my studio!" I pointed to the mess. "Make sure you clean all this shit up before you leave too! I told Grandma I would look after your hardheaded ass, and I swear I'm trying, but you're making it hard, Tre."

He sighed, hanging his head low. "I know, and that's my bad. I'll do better."

"Good." I released a yawn. "Now, let me get the fuck on, so I can try to get some sleep before we start auditions tomorrow.

Tre and I were shooting a movie about our life. We had been through so much shit and still lived to tell our story. Every bitch in town wanted to fuck with the Lattimore brothers, and every nigga wanted to be us, quite naturally. So, it was only right that we created a movie to showcase the things we went through to get to the successful place that we were in our lives currently.

"Aight, bruh. I'll see you tomorrow. Love you."

"I love you too, lil' nigga!" I pulled my brother in for a handshake and a hug.

He hated when I called him a little nigga because the irony was that he was actually, in fact, bigger than me. Trevin had a different complexion than I had since we had different fathers. He was dark-skinned with locs and a pot belly, but the ladies loved it. This nigga was barely taller than me, standing at six foot four, was tatted up damn near everywhere, including our granny's name tattooed above his eyebrow, had gold slugs, and one of the freshest dress codes I had ever seen. My lil' bro was really that nigga—I mean, after me, that is.

"Get yo' shit together."

"I will. I'm telling you, nigga. I got you."

I nodded before leaving, hopping in my car, and heading home.

* * *

"What the fuck?"

I walked into my bedroom, and in my bed was my ex-girlfriend, Faylen.

"Faylen, what in the fuck are you doing here? Don't you have a husband to get back to?"

She and I simply didn't work out, but I never knew she fell out of love with me until I proposed at a party in front of all our friends and family. She said no, stormed off crying, and I was left looking stupid. When I finally got a chance to chop it up with her, she told me that she was in love with another man, and she was leaving me for him.

I would be lying if I said that shit didn't hurt me to the core, but honestly, I always felt like my situation with Faylen helped make me into a better man. I started throwing myself into my work, and that was how I ended up with a very successful recording studio.

I left relationships alone for good, only sleeping with women here and there, and just focusing on myself and my bag. I was not interested in seeing her, being with her again, or even sleeping with her again. So, the fact that she was in my bed wearing lingerie was blowing my mind.

She and I only fucked once after they got married, but that was ages ago. I felt weird as fuck going from her main nigga to her side nigga, so I began to ignore all texts and calls from her until now.

"H-hey, baby," she stammered, hopping up from the bed.

I would also be lying if I said I didn't love the way she looked in the lingerie set she had on. It was hugging her body in all the right places.

The titty area was cut out, so her nipples were hard and standing fully at attention.

I must have startled her, seeing how she jumped, but I should have been the one startled because she was there uninvited. I didn't even see a car outside, so that confused the hell out of me.

"Where's your car, and why are you here? Matter of fact, how did you get in here?"

"I caught an Uber since I wanted to surprise you, and through the keypad silly, remember you gave me the code the last time we made love?" She slowly yet seductively walked over to me and snaked her hands up my chest. She wrapped her arms around my neck like I was her prey.

If I wasn't so against falling back into her trap, I might have indulged, but because I was in a different headspace than I once was when I was with Faylen, I grabbed her hands, snatched them from around my neck, and gently shoved her backward. She looked confused as to why I was behaving the way I was, but again, she embarrassed the fuck out of me, and I didn't do do-overs.

"I thought you would be happy to see me." She crossed her arms over her big ass titties, and her mad face made my dick jump, so I had to look away.

"You gotta go, and I'm not even about to—" She reached for me, and I moved back. "Faylen, come on now. What the fuck is you on?"

"I'm tryna be on you, but you're trippin'."

"You need to go see 'bout yo' nigga. You know, the one you turned down my proposal for?"

She sighed, running her fingers through her hair. Faylen was gorgeous, no doubt, but her ways were wicked.

Any other nigga whose proposal got turned down probably would have dragged her ass out of their crib by now, but I had a soft spot for her. Not in the sense of us working shit out, but just in the sense of me not doing her as dirty as she did me. Lucky for her, I wasn't a tit-for-tat type of nigga.

"That's not what happened, Assad! You and I just weren't working out. We were in such a weird space and—"

"No, you were in a weird space. I had no idea about the way you felt until you turned down my proposal. Either way, I'm not having this conversation with you tonight or any other night because I simply don't give a fuck. Why do you think we fucked once after you got married to the next nigga? How do you think that made me feel? Why do you think I stopped answering your calls and text messages, huh?"

"I'm sorry, okay! I should have never embarrassed you like that. Maybe I should have accepted your proposal and then denied you in the privacy of our own home instead of in front of everybody. Is that what you want to hear, Assad?" she yelled.

I couldn't do shit but laugh because if that's what she thought I wanted to hear, then she really didn't know me at all like I thought she did. Stepping closer to her so I could make sure she could hear me loud and clear, I got all up in her face. She didn't even flinch. But, then again, I wasn't expecting her to and didn't really give a damn if she did or not. I just wanted to make sure she heard me.

"What I would have wanted from the woman who I expected to spend the rest of my life with was for her to be honest with me about her feelings. You ain't shit but a user. As a matter of fact, you and Trevin's baby mama should be the best of fucking friends. I had enough money to take care of you... to take care of us at the time. You left me for someone who had more money than me at that point in my life, but now that I have one of the biggest record labels, a big ass house, a big ass bank account, I drive expensive cars, wear expensive clothes, and all that other shit, you trying to backpedal to me? Bitch, please see yourself the fuck out of my house and out of my life for good with your using ass!"

"Bitch?" Her mouth flew open, and she reached to slap me, but I grabbed her arm and threw her back so hard that she fell on her ass.

As she lay on the floor, she looked up at me with tears in her eyes. "Really, Assad? That's how we rocking?"

I nodded. "Straight like that, now please leave."

She helped herself up, and her tears cascaded down her face as she quickly grabbed her things and stormed out of my room. I had to fight the urge to follow her, apologize, and hold her as I sat on the bed, now in a fucked-up ass mood.

"Fuck!"

Chapter Five

DE'ARRA

"Damn, you cooked?" Paige asked as she yawned and wiped her eyes.

I slept in the living room after we stayed up half the night, drinking wine, bashing niggas, and just bonding.

When I rolled over, my stomach immediately started talking, so after showering, freshening up with my toiletries that I always left over there, and throwing on some of Paige's clothes, I started on breakfast. She didn't have much in the fridge, so I made cheesy spinach omelets for us.

"And did. But, bitch, don't come up in here yawning, knowing you need to handle that dragon breath."

Quickly covering her mouth, Paige said, "Girl, fuck you. I'm headed to the bathroom now. I just stopped in the kitchen first to make sure you weren't burning my shit down."

Placing my hand on my hip after flipping the omelet, I turned to her. "Don't even try me like that. I can cook. Matter of fact, I can throw down! You, on the other hand, not so much."

She scoffed, rolling her eyes. "Yeah, okay. I'll let you think that. I'll go get freshened up, and then I'll be... bitch, are you wearing my clothes?"

Taunting her, I gave her a spin. "Don't I look damn good?"

She smirked. "You look aight, but make sure to return my shit. You know how you do."

"Girl, don't nobody wanna keep your raggedy clothes."

Paige waved me off. "If they're so raggedy, then take them off, hoe."

"You're just mad that I look better in your clothes than you ever could."

Paige flipped me the bird and started walking off. "Whatever. Let me go shower and get myself together."

"Oh, shit," I mumbled to myself. "Wait. Are you doing anything today? I completely forgot Izzy told me last night that I have to go meet that Assad guy today, and I really don't want to go alone," I whined.

She stopped her stride and turned around to face me. "Yeah, I don't have anything planned. I'm off today, but I did want to slide by the shop to make sure shit is in order. I mean, I guess I can just call PooPoo to check on things, and I'll slide with you."

"I still can't believe she wants people to call her PooPoo," I said in reference to a woman who was twice our age.

She was cool and had worked for my sister for a few years, but she had the ugliest nickname I had ever heard. PooPoo also managed the shop when my sis wasn't around.

I continued. "Anyway, thank God you're coming with me." I wiped the imaginary sweat from my forehead. "I didn't want to go alone but would've had no choice if you said no. Thanks."

"I got you, sis." She winked before walking off, dragging her feet the whole damn time.

"Girl, pick your feet up!" I shouted as I grabbed a plate from the cabinet to plate the first omelet that I'd finished.

"Girl, this my shit. If you don't like it, you can leave, hoe!"

I laughed and set the plate to the side as my mind slowly but surely drifted to the meet-up I was dreading. I might have been holding it together well on the outside, but on the inside, I was freaking out. I hated that this shit was happening so fast. Knowing Izzy, he probably knew about this shit with Assad for a while and was just now telling me at the last minute like he did with every damn thing else. I hated when he did that. Either way, I wanted to just lie down, relax, and not have to worry about this big ass mess Izzy had dragged us both into.

Well, I guess that won't be happening.

* * *

"What the hell?"

Paige and I pulled up to the address Izzy sent me, which for one, was far as shit from the crib. After driving almost forty-five minutes to Buford Highway from Fulton Industrial, I was pissed to see that the parking lot was on swole. The place I was supposed to meet Assad at had a line wrapped damn near around the building twice.

"Is she bending over, showing her pussy print?" Paige asked with her face practically glued to the window. "Oh shit, she hit a split!"

I sighed, shaking my head while looking for a parking spot. I didn't know much about cars, and I wasn't materialistic at all, but I spotted a white Rolls Royce whipping into the parking lot.

"Damn, that car is sexy!"

Paige had pissed me off lowkey because she was so worried about what was going on instead of helping me look for parking.

"Girl, fuck that. Do you see any parking spots on your side? If not, I'm definitely leaving, and Izzy can kiss my ass."

"Nope," She quickly replied, and I was sure she probably half looked.

Shaking my head again, I spotted one right on the front and quickly stepped on the gas.

"Oh, I see one right here."

I was two seconds from zooming into the spot when the Rolls Royce that had circled the small and crowded parking lot came around and tried to bully me out of the space. Their windows were tinted, and I wasn't sure they even saw me cursing their ass out, so I rolled my window down.

"This is my spot, asshole! Get your own!"

I expected them to move, but instead, they sat still, not even bothering to roll down the window.

"Hello!" I spat, but still no response, so I put my car in park, snatched off my seatbelt, and hopped out.

Normally, I'd never be this impulsive, but due to the circumstances, I just wanted to meet this Assad nigga and leave just as fast as I had come. All this extra shit was blowing my high, and I didn't even smoke.

I walked around to the driver's side and started banging on their window. "I have things to do, so can you move your car?"

I expected the window to come down, so I stepped back and crossed my arms. Instead, the car door to the driver's side slowly opened, and a very beautiful man hopped out with a unit on his face. He was taller than I expected, towering over me, and he had some meat on his bones, but in a good way. Swallowing the lump in my throat, I didn't back down as I heard Paige say something. I hadn't even realized she hopped out of the car as well.

"Bitch, is you crazy? You almost hit my shit, and then you—"

SLAP!

In that moment, I didn't give a damn that he was very good looking. I slapped fire out of his ass. He was brown-skinned, about six foot three, and looking like a mix between Nipsey Hussle and Dave East, with a massive, neatly trimmed beard that I wanted to stroke. His hair was long and braided into two very neat braids that came past his shoulders. His lips, which were now balled up, were a dark brown color on the top and a beautiful shade of pink on the bottom. He was tatted up, but nothing too crazy. I couldn't necessarily see his full body, but I saw a wrist, neck, and arm sleeve. His eyes were a gorgeous hazel green.

Although he was cursing me out, and the veins were popping from his neck, especially after I slapped him, I peeped that his teeth were straight as hell, his breath that blew in the wind was fresh, and he could clearly dress his ass off. It looked like his whole outfit could pay my rent for about two to three months.

With a balled-up fist, he stepped closer to me, bringing me back from the trance his fine, rude ass had me in.

Paige got between us.

"I'm so sorry, Assad. I know you don't know me, but please excuse my sister. She's normally much nicer than this." She looked at me, giving me the eye, but I didn't give a damn about that.

I was shocked to find out he was Assad, but that didn't make too much of a difference.

Pushing my sister to the side, I said, "No, don't excuse this asshole! He tried to steal my spot and then called me out my name! Fuck him!"

"De'arra... remember why we're here. You can't just..." Paige was giving me signals with her eyes, but I furiously looked away and back over to this fine specimen.

"I didn't try to steal shit. This is my parking spot. I own the parking lot and almost all the lounges in this bitch!"

When he said that, I literally had nothing to say because if he did, in fact, own the parking lot, then my dumb ass just embarrassed myself for no reason.

"Listen, my sister came here to meet you today. She's uh... Izzy's girlfriend. Again, she didn't mean any harm. It was a simple mistake. Please don't kill her, Mr. Lattimore."

"Bitch, shut up." I nudged her, and she threw up her hands in mock surrender.

"What? I'm tryna save you from having your eyeballs, kneecaps, and elbows served on a platter back to Izzy."

Assad snickered, which meant he had a sense of humor.

"Bruh, we got shit to do. Wrap this shit up!" A big nigga hopped out of the car, causing the crowd to go wild and Paige to gasp behind me.

I didn't know who he was, but everyone else did. He was very handsome and looked exactly like Assad but thicker with all kinds of expensive chains, rings, and shit on.

"Oh, my God! Tre Bang! I wanna have your baby!" some woman shouted, then stuck out her tongue.

This Tre Bang character winked at the woman as security came out and practically surrounded the car.

"So, you're in a relationship with fuck boy Izzy, huh?" Assad licked his luscious lips as I placed my hand on my hip and caught a whole different attitude.

"Izzy is not a fuck boy, but yes, that's my man. Why, what's up?" Izzy wasn't my favorite person in the world right now, but I wasn't going to bad mouth him to this nigga I didn't know.

Assad looked me up and down. "I completely forgot about our meet-up today, but uh..." He held his hand out for mine.

Like a fool, I placed my hand in his, and he spun me around to get a good look at me. "I apologize sincerely for calling you out of your name. That's not even my style."

I smacked my lips. "Mhm."

"Forgive me, baby." He was laying it on thick, but I peeped, so I slid my hand out of his.

"Yeah, whatever. All is forgiven, but when will we have time to talk since you got all of this going on today?" I pointed to the crowd of people surrounding the building.

"Look, just come inside and chill out for a lil' bit, mama. We're having auditions for our new film, but my people will make sure you and your friend are taken care of."

"This is actually my sister, Paige, and I'm uh... I'm De'arra."

"Nice to meet you both, but we really have to go inside. We're running behind, so y'all follow me."

I nodded as the security ushered the four of us toward the entrance, but once we reached the door, I said, "Wait. What about my car? I didn't get a chance to—"

"You're good, mama. My people will move your car and mine."

I sighed, looking back at Paige, who looked like a kid in a candy store. "Okay."

We made our way inside, and photographers snapped all kinds of pictures of us as we were led to the back, where a large table was set up. We walked past so many damn people, and I was annoyed because I just knew this was going to be a long day.

Chapter Six

PAIGE

De'arra and I were in the middle of tearing up our food when Assad came over.

"Let me get a piece," he said, clearly flirting with my sister. I couldn't help but laugh because one thing she hated was sharing her food.

We were all taking a break after seeing so many horrible ass auditions. I was so glad I wasn't a part of selecting people for the film because this was truly a shit show.

Aside from the auditions, I couldn't keep my eyes off Trevin. He was so damn cute in person. I saw him stealing glances at me as well, so at least I knew we were on one accord when it came to attraction. However, with his fame and status, I was sure he was used to women falling all over him, throwing it at him on a daily basis, and just making it too easy for him.

"Excuse you, Mr. 'I own the parking lot and all the lounges in it.' You need to get your own food. I don't share, and I don't even know you!" De'arra spat, causing me to snicker.

"My sister does not play when it comes to her food, so that's a little tip for you since you're supposed to be spending time with each other for the next few weeks," I chimed in, and she looked at me happily, as if she were glad I intervened.

"Speaking of the next few weeks, can we please just discuss this deal so I can go?"

Assad looked around before looking back over at De'arra. "We can, but I wanted to do that in private, mama."

She hopped up from her seat like it was on fire. "Okay, well, let's go somewhere private then."

He nodded before walking off. De'arra rolled her eyes and followed suit as I chuckled. Picking up my fork, I went to town on my salmon Alfredo.

"Please sign my titties, Tre Bang!" A woman yelled as she ran full speed past security at him.

My mouth literally dropped open when I looked up and saw a woman with her titties exposed, practically attacking Trevin. He looked mortified because this lady had to be at least in her mid-fifties, but she looked good for her age, in my opinion.

"Man, what the fuck?" he said, pushing the woman off. "Y'all muthafuckas must not want y'all jobs because how the fuck she get back here?"

I chuckled as security pulled her away.

He sucked his teeth and looked over at me. "Man, that shit ain't funny."

Once my laughter died down and I was actually able to contain myself, I said, "You never know. She could have been your sugar mama, and you just missed out on a blessing."

He shook his head, making a disgusted face. "Hell nah. Shawty not even my speed. Besides, I got my own fucking money. I don't need a sugar mama."

I smiled. "Mmm, well, excuse me."

"You're excused with your pretty ass."

I blushed, looking away and getting back to my food to avoid eye contact.

"Damn, mama, so I can give a compliment but can't get one back?"

I kissed my teeth, looking back over at him. "You know you're fly. You and I both know that. You don't even need me to tell you that."

T. MICHELLE

He playfully brushed his shoulders off. "You know what? You might be onto something there," he kidded, and we both laughed.

I expected him to be this rude ass, conceited big boy. Instead, he was funny and, so far, seemed to be a gentle giant. He stepped closer into my space.

"Exactly. Give me my props, though, because I already knew that. With you being a rapper and a very well-known one at that, the many women falling at your feet should be a daily reminder."

"Despite what you think, women fall at my feet, and I've entertained a very small few. But a nigga ain't no hoe or nothing like that."

"I never said you were, love. I'm just saying that you are what I'd like to consider every woman's dream. Good looking, talented, paid, and slanging good dick."

Crossing his arms, he licked his lips and eyed me with a smirk. "Who said I have good dick? My shit could be the size of a peanut."

I leaned forward on the table. "Other than that big ass print you're sporting, your crazy ass baby mama could probably vouch for you. I mean, she is always doing interviews with *TheShadyGlobe,* and from the looks of things, she ain't turning you loose for nobody."

"Man, I ain't with that crazy ass girl. We just have kids together and co-parent. That's it."

I shrugged, sitting back in my seat. "You may not be with her, but that settles my point. You got something she loves, and it ain't just the money, boo."

"Oh, my God! I'm going to throw up!" Chaz, a gay guy who I learned was one of the producers of the film, came running into the back, holding his stomach.

"Nigga, you better the fuck not!" Trevin chastised Chaz as he held onto his mouth and then quickly leaned on the nearby wall.

"What's wrong?" a few members of the crew and I asked all at the same time.

"Two women are out there eating each other out! Not only does it smell like tuna, but they said they won't stop until Tre Bang himself comes out and tells them to. I have never seen anything like that in my life!"

I giggled. He was being so dramatic.

"Cheer up, nigga. It's just pussy. It doesn't even bite or anything. You should have joined in and got a little nibble," Trevin joked, but Chaz was not feeling his joke at all.

Chaz flipped him the bird as Trevin called his security over. "Handle that for me."

The security nodded before quickly going to handle the problem. I was shocked that he didn't go see the free freak show for himself.

"You're not into bitches eating each other out?" I was curious yet nosy at the same time.

He paused, silently examining my face before saying, "Is that a bruise on your eye, mama?"

I quickly stood as if my seat had electrocuted my ass and excused myself. Not only was it hot today, but it was also a little toasty in the area we were in. It was very possible that my makeup had shifted, so I needed to quickly fix that. If Trevin could see the bruise Millz left on my face, then other people probably could as well.

"Damn," I said to myself as I looked in the bathroom mirror. My makeup had definitely moved around a little. I was still pretty as fuck, regardless, but a little touch-up wouldn't hurt.

DE'ARRA

"Wait, so you live here? In the lounge?" I looked around the room he took me to, and there was a damn bed, television, and a few other things that made me believe he lived at his place of business.

"Why would you ask me a dumbass question like that?" he snapped, causing my head to jerk to the side as I kissed my teeth.

"If you're going to be anything in this world, be fucking for real. There's a whole bed in here, a TV, a mini fridge, and..." I walked over to the bathroom and looked inside. "A shower and condom wrapper in this here trash can as well. So, again, be fucking for real. If you live here, then just say that."

He smirked. "First of all, no, I don't live here with your nosy ass. This is my place of business... well, one of them. A lot of people don't know all of what I have my hands in, and I like it that way. As far as the used condoms, that ain't got shit to do with me. Someone else stayed here last night, not me. I have a home and a bed that I sleep in every night. I'm barely ever here, and nine times out of ten, I'm at the studio. The bed and all this other shit here is a convenience, but don't get it twisted, baby. A nigga really got money for real. I don't have to sleep at my lounge."

"Mhm... well, anyway, let's just talk about the real reason I'm here and the reason we even came back here." Shifting my weight one foot, I continued as I leaned against the TV stand. "My boyfriend said he owes you a shit ton of money, and y'all made this dumb ass deal for me to be with you for the next three weeks. Is that correct?"

He nodded, so I continued. "Okay, cool. So, when do we start? What does this entail, and you do know you're not getting any pussy from me, right?"

Looking me up and down, the expression on his face was a little hard to read, so I remained quiet, waiting for him to speak.

"Oh, I see you got a mouth on you."

I nodded with my lips pursed before crossing my arms. "And do!"

"Well, first, let me say this. If I wanted pussy from you, I could have it, so let's just start there. Secondly, I'm not in the business of taking another black man's life over some money that I have plenty of. Yes, he owes me, and yes, I would prefer my fucking money back. However, he insisted that he exchange his most prized possession, which would be you, to settle the debt."

"Wait!" I threw my hands up. "You're telling me that Izzy, the man I've been in a relationship with for the past four years, offered me up to you to pay for the 100k he owes you and not the other way around? He made it seem like you're oh so dangerous, and if I didn't do it, there would be consequences."

I couldn't believe my ears. I felt betrayed all over again. He had to be out of his mind and smoking that stuff to even think that offering me up was an option, to begin with.

Assad nodded, and now he looked confused. "That nigga told you otherwise? If so, I don't fuck with that because he could have been man enough to tell you the truth. He owes me and has nothing to give me in return. From my research, he don't have shit in his name, not even a house or a car, and his credit is fucked. That's the kind of niggas you fuck with?"

"No, that's the kind of man I used to fuck with because I swear, after this, I'm good on him. He had my heart racing all fast and made me think you were going to kill him over this money."

"Nah, not my style, but if you're going to leave him anyway, why even go through with it? Why not make that nigga figure out how to get me my money?"

"Because this is chess, not checkers, and I'm going to make him sweat a little. I want him to see that he practically pushed me into the arms of another man. A good looking, rich one at that."

Assad chuckled. "Not you tryna use me like I'm a piece of meat, shawty. Now, that's fucked up. I thought we were better than that." He reached up and grabbed a piece of my hair, twirling it around his finger.

I scoffed. "I don't even know you."

I pushed his hand away because, quite frankly, his big, strong hands being too close to me made my pussy jump. Even though he was only playing with my hair, my nasty ass was thinking about him playing with my pussy. I had already peeped that his nails were nice and clean, too, which was a plus.

Girl, stop. You are not fucking this man!

"Yet. Stop leaving off the 'yet' part. You don't know me yet, but that's coming soon."

I laughed. "What does that even mean?"

"It means whatever you want it to mean, mama. You're mine for the next three weeks, but I'm not into making you do anything you don't want to do. For the most part, I'll be at work. You can come with me to meetings and shit like that. We can hang out, get to know each other, fuck, or whatever your heart desires, shawty. This ain't some shit I do often. In fact, this is a first for me, so I'm just going with the flow."

I smirked. "I like how you tried to ease in the fucking part when I just told you I'm not giving up this pretty pussy."

"Oh, she's pretty, just like you? Don't tempt me with a good time." I playfully pushed his chest.

"I'm kidding. She looks like a gremlin."

He threw his hands up in mock surrender. "Oh, you're good, then. Keep that ugly motherfucker away from me."

We both burst out laughing as a knock at the door startled us.

"Come in!" Assad shouted.

A few moments later, Trevin poked his head inside. "Aye, bruh, we're about to start back up."

"Aight, give me a sec."

"Bet," Trevin replied, closing the door behind him.

"I have a question before we go back out there."

Crossing his arms, he placed his hand under his chin, giving me his undivided attention and practically staring into my soul. "Shoot."

I froze for a moment, feeling like I was in the sunken place.

Lord, this man is beautiful.

"So, do I have to actually live with you for the next three weeks, or just like spend time with you?"

"I mean, the deal is that you're mine, and any woman who has the honor of being mine... well, she needs to share a roof with me... her *man*." He winked at me before walking off.

The second he left the room, I had to fan myself.

"He better stop before I put this pussy in his mouth," I mumbled to myself before following him out.

Chapter Seven

TREVIN

"Stop fucking calling me, Kim! You know I'm busy, and you're not even calling about Cassie or Carmelo." Having kids with Kim was the worst thing I could have done.

Carmelo was almost three, while little Cassie had just turned one. I disliked my baby mama a lot, but I loved the fuck out of my kids. They were blessings, and I'd never treat them differently just because their mama was a damn fool. She had been on stalker type shit ever since I started back fucking her, and that was my mistake.

Then, when my music started going viral, all of a sudden, she wanted to raise the kids as a family, and she kept hollering about how my money was her money. I didn't know where the fuck she got that from, especially since she wasn't with me shooting in the gym. I broke her off here and there, but the shit was getting out of control now.

"Nigga, bye. You know why I'm calling, and it does kind of have something to do with the kids. I need some money to get my hair, nails, and feet done, plus some spending money for the mall. I need some new clothes, and I'll make sure to grab something for them as well."

I shook my head. "Do you hear yourself right now? Kim, you're too old for this shit. You act like you don't know what the fuck be going on.

You literally just asked me for money to get a whole bunch of shit done for yourself and that you'll make sure to grab some shit for my kids. That don't even make no sense, and it's very obvious that your priorities are fucked up, Kim!"

With Kim being older than me, I always expected more from her. But I guess some things would never change about her, regardless of age.

"Priorities? I am their sole provider, and I do for them every chance I get. But, damn, I can't make sure I look good too? I mean, how would that look anyway, with Tre Bang's baby mama out in these streets, looking like a hot mess?"

I sucked my teeth as I headed for the bathroom. "You're clearly not hearing me if you're trying to justify the dumb shit you're saying. Yes, my kids live with you, but you don't even work. That's my money paying for the rent, clothes, shoes, food, and all of that. All you do is hold out your fucking hands. I'm not even yo' nigga, and it's not my responsibility to make sure you have your hair and all that shit done. You trippin' for real."

I was seeing red and not even paying attention. I bumped right into shawty, and it was then that I realized I didn't even know her name.

"Oh, my God! I'm so sorry. I have got to get out of the habit of walking with my head down." She smiled. She was so fucking gorgeous, a nigga's dick jumped. We were so close that her titties were up against my chest, and she smelled like fruity ass women's perfume—good enough to eat.

"You're good, mama. I wasn't paying attention either." I laughed right before all hell broke loose.

Kim started spazzing and yelling in my ear, making me remember that I was on the phone with her dumbass to begin with.

"Who the fuck is 'good,' and nigga you got me fucked up! I'm coming up there!"

"Don't bring yo' ass up here, Kim. What I'm doing or who I'm talking to is none of your—"

Click

Kim hung up on me, and I couldn't do shit but shake my head as nameless giggled.

"What's your name, Ms. Giggles?" I held out my hand for her, but she declined it by pushing my hand away. My brows rose in amusement.

"Paige, but it seems like there's trouble in paradise, so let me gone on and ease out of your way. Sounds like 'Kim' is coming up here, and although a bitch can fight, I'm not in the mood to do so. Excuse me."

She slipped past me, and I got a good look at her backside. She was definitely caked up. I was intrigued by her and hoped that Kim didn't bring her ass up there. I was having a good day and wasn't in the mood to deal with her shit. She was always on my ass like we had titles to one another other than BD and BM, which pissed me clean off. Assad was always getting on me for still fucking Kim. I always brushed his ass off about a lot of the shit he said, but I was really starting to see over the past month or so why this wasn't a good idea.

That's what you get for thinking with your dick.

* * *

After wrapping up auditions for the day, I was exhausted. We had a few people come and really show out, but for the most part, we mainly got wanna be upcoming rappers trying to shoot their shot, people who couldn't act their way out of a paper bag, and a plethora of hungry groupie ass hoes trying to bag either my brother or myself.

The sun was practically going down as we wrapped everything up. We'd have to have another meeting or two to look over all the submissions and in-person audition tapes.

"Bruh, we saw some pretty okay people today, but we didn't find anyone to play Angel. Well, at least in my opinion. What do you think?"

I agreed with my brother on that one. Angel was literally an angel—my ex, who passed away due to being at the wrong place at the wrong time while carrying my seed, who also didn't make it.

I honestly think that one of the reasons I ended up with Kim so quickly and locked her down was that I was trying to fill the hole in my heart that Angel left when she passed away.

I was so in love with her and ready to get on one knee to marry her and give her and my son the best life they ever could dream of until tragedy happened. With us doing a movie about our life, it only made

T. MICHELLE

sense to include Angel because she played a big part in shaping the person I was today.

Angel was a no-nonsense type of person, and she always put me in check. She was also very sweet, caring and would give you the shirt off her back if she needed to. She was gorgeous, fucked me and sucked me better than any woman ever had, and would lay down her life for me.

I wish I was there to protect her at the time of her shooting. I would have for sure taken that bullet for her. It wasn't a day that went by that I didn't think about Angel or Trevin Junior.

Kim was so different from Angel in every way. It must've been her smooth butter pecan skin, fat ass, triple D titties, and mouth that pulled me in. I mean, her head wasn't hitting on shit as far as Angel was concerned, but it was definitely getting the job done. I liked the fact that in the beginning, she catered to my every need, waiting on me hand and foot like I was a king or some shit. She agreed to do whatever I wanted, never put up a fight, didn't argue, and was very submissive. Angel would never do no shit like that. She would rather tell you the truth than a lie and would never bite her tongue.

Kim really fooled me, and I was still pissed that I didn't see she was running game on me.

"Nah, you're right. I didn't see anyone who could play Angel and actually do her justice."

"What about me?" Paige stood and walked over to the table where we had excerpts of the script printed out.

"Wait... you've been here all day and never mentioned one word to me about being an actress?"

I wasn't sure how good she was, but appearance-wise, she was about the same height and build as Angel.

"Well, I'm not quite an actress. I own my own hair salon, but... I did some background work in the past and took two acting classes. I've yet to show off what I learned. Plus, I've been here all day, and at this point, I practically know the lines."

I looked over at Assad, who gave me a 'why the fuck not' look, so I agreed to let her audition.

"Aight, go ahead, mama."

Paige smiled and glanced down at the paper in her hand. A few moments later, she set the paper down and held her hand out for me.

"What happened?"

"Be my scene partner, silly. Plus, you're playing yourself in the movie anyway, so you might as well do the scene with me."

I placed my hand into her small, soft hand as she pulled me around the table. I couldn't even remember the last time I held a woman's hand.

Before I could dwell on it, she started reading her lines as if she were Angel.

"Do you wanna be with me or not, Trevin?"

Clearing my throat, I said, "Bae, you know I wanna be with you. I wanna be there for you and my baby. How could you even ask me something like that?"

"You don't act like it." Crossing her arms, she looked away from me. "You love the streets more than you love me, and I just... I can't compete."

"Bae, look at me." Grabbing her chin, I turned her face to look at me. "Bae... I promise you that I'll do better for you and our unborn. You just gotta have faith in me."

"I do. Trust me, I really do, but actions speak louder than words, Trevin."

"Baby, you have my word."

"Mhm." She smacked her lips before playfully rolling her eyes. "If you're really serious, then seal it with a kiss."

Wrapping my arm around her back, I pulled her closer to my body. "You always did love my kisses."

I licked my lips, preparing for the kiss in the scene as Paige yanked me up by my shirt. "No, you love my kisses. Don't play."

I laughed. "You're right about that."

Leaning down to meet her halfway, my lips crashed into hers. For a very hot second, I felt some weird shit in my stomach, but it was hard to explain. I forgot we were acting as my tongue slipped into her mouth. She allowed it, and before I knew it, we were engaged in a very intense make-out session and shit. But it didn't even feel like a nigga was kissing a stranger. It felt real.

We both jumped apart when we heard clapping and cheering.

"I think we found our Angel, man!" Assad shouted as he stood up excitedly.

"Yeah, sissy, you did so good. I felt like I was watching the actual movie. You both killed it."

"Thanks, boo!" Paige said to her sister before winking at her. She then smiled, now looking back and forth between Assad and me. "So, does that mean I got the part?"

A nigga was still stuck from that kiss, so I didn't know what to say. I just nodded.

Paige squealed, jumping into my arms, but her moment was short lived.

PAIGE

"Bitch, get your hands off my man before you end up at the morgue with a toe tag, hoe!"

Everyone's heads literally turned at the same time, and that's when I saw Kim, Trevin's baby mama. I had never seen her in person, and she was actually cuter than I thought. But, of course, she didn't have shit on me.

I hated that she was ruining my moment. I couldn't believe I was chosen for the film. I was literally on cloud nine for a very short time before Kim barged in with some girl.

"Kim, don't come in here with all of that," Assad scolded her.

She completely ignored him as if he were a measly insect flying past her ear and proceeded to march up to Trevin and me. Kim stopped directly in front of us and tried to raise her hand to do what, I'm not sure, but Trevin stepped in front of me, which I took note of in my head.

"Move, Trevin. I'm not going to hit your little whore."

I simply laughed from behind Trevin's back as my sister chimed in. "You're right, baby girl. You're not going to hit my sister because I will lay you out, pussy hoe. Play with it!"

Kim looked at her and rolled her eyes but didn't dare say another word.

"It's not even that type of party, Kim. You knew I was down here doing auditions for the movie, which is why I couldn't get the kids this weekend. You also know that I'm acting in the movie. So, I'm not sure what all you saw, but she and I were acting out a scene."

Why is he explaining himself to her?

"Oh, I saw everything and nigga, I'm not stupid." Kim tried to shove Trevin backward, but he didn't even move an inch when she pushed him. "Tell her how you ate my pussy last night."

"What?" Both Assad and I said at the same time.

"Man, bitch stop lying!" Trevin was pissed. I could see it all on his face.

I quickly wiped my lips and threw up the deuces.

"Come on, sis, let's dip because this here ain't got shit to do with us."

"Bitch?" Kim said, but the second I tried to walk off, Trevin grabbed me.

"Nah, don't go. They're leaving." He gave me a look that read he sincerely apologized for the bullshit.

I sighed as the guy who I learned was Skooly, their main security, walked over. I could tell this was something that happened often because Skooly didn't even look fazed.

"I can't believe this! My friend has been nothing but loyal to you. She has been down for you since the beginning, and this is how you choose to repay her? She gave you two beautiful kids, and you have the audacity to keep playing in her face!" Kim's friend shouted before turning to Assad. "And you... I don't appreciate what went down last night, and now I see why you've been acting funny with me." She pointed to my sister.

De'arra laughed, also clapping her hands, which tickled me. "Girl, you want an award for that performance?"

"No, but I want an award for beating your ass!" The friend charged at De'arra, who hopped up just in time. The girl missed, but De'arra never missed. She hit ol' girl with a two-piece.

"Oh, shit!" Assad shouted as he kicked his chair back and jumped between the two as best he could.

Skooly grabbed the friend as I eyed Kim. We never had to jump a bitch because we didn't play that shit. So, if Kim decided to be on some jumping shit, I was ready to be all over her ass. I slipped out of my shoes and took my earrings off.

"Get the fuck off my friend!" Kim shouted at Skooly before beating him in the back of the head and back.

"Yo, Skooly, take them outta here, man," Trevin advised.

With one swift motion, he picked Kim up as well and escorted them out.

"Fuck you, Trevin! You gon' pay for this!"

The truth of the matter was that I had a lot that I wanted to say. However, he wasn't my man, and in fact, probably never would be. He had too much going on, and so did I. So, whatever this flirting shit was that we had going on today, it was probably going to be nipped in the bud, especially after what just happened with his baby mama. I hated to fuck with niggas who had kids for this exact reason.

Chapter Eight

KIM

"Girl, fuck him. You can do so much better than him," Myra said as we got to the car after Skooly's fat neck ass threw us out again.

Sometimes, I hated being so small. That nigga manhandled us and easily picked us up. We didn't even stand a chance.

I was lowkey mad at her ass. "Girl, shut up and get in the fucking car because all of this could have been avoided."

Myra's head whipped in my direction as she hit the button to unlock her car. I angrily slid into the passenger seat as she hopped in, going off on me. "Bitch, I know you ain't mad at me for fighting that hoe. She was being sarcastic and sitting way too close to my man. I know they got some shit going on, so don't blame me for getting active. The second we walked in, and you saw ol 'girl lip-locking with Trevin, you should've been on her ass too!"

I shook my head as she cranked the car, but I stopped her. "I'm not ready to leave."

She smiled. "Oh, you ready to get active now?" She turned the car back off.

"No, it's not even that. I just wanna talk to him for real."

"Girl, fuck talking. He already showed you what it is. Nigga can fuck on you when he wants but still gets to fuck on other girls too? If you did the same, it would be a problem, though."

"I mean, technically, I am, Myra. You know I'm sleeping with—"

Myra cut me off midsentence. "Bitch, they're walking out now. Let's go."

This was one of the main reasons I didn't like to bring Myra around. She was my best friend, and I loved her to death, but she was always too rowdy for me. Yes, I was definitely on ten before we got there, and it upset me to see Trevin kissing that woman, but I wasn't trying to fight. All I wanted was for us to be together, and I didn't feel like that was asking too much.

Myra threw her things down in the car and hopped out with the quickness. We weren't parked too far from Assad's car. Trevin must've ridden with him because I didn't see his car anywhere. They were laughing and talking with the same two women from inside.

"Round two, hoe!" Myra yelled and attacked the woman closest to Assad, the same one she was fighting inside.

She looked very familiar to me, but I couldn't put my finger on it. I didn't know her personally, but her face just stood out to me for some reason.

All I simply tried to do was separate them, but I guess the woman she was with thought I was trying to jump in. So, the next thing I knew, the four of us were scrapping like dogs.

I got some good licks in, that's for sure, but someone punched me in my damn mouth and split my lip. It was probably Myra's ass since she was swinging her arms so wildly.

This time, instead of Skooly breaking us up, Trevin snatched me up and threw me to the ground, hurting the fuck out of my wrist, ass, and my feelings.

"Just fucking stop, Kim! Got damn! The fuck is your problem?" Trevin very seldom raised his voice, and I could see the annoyance practically oozing from his body. He looked fed up with me for sure, but my attention was soon put on Myra when she got knocked on her ass right next to me, falling to the ground like a log.

Myra moaned and groaned.

DE'ARRA

"Girl, are you slow? I don't even know you, and I'm not even fucking yo' nigga. But guess what? Now I am, hoe!" Paige shouted as I pushed Assad off me.

I did not sign up for this shit and couldn't wait to tell Izzy off. This was a damn circus act, and Kim was the damn ringleader.

Rolling up in there, starting stuff with both my sister and me over Trevin and Assad, was ridiculous. Then, from the looks of things, Trevin couldn't care less about Kim. He threw her to the ground as if she meant nothing. She sat there leaking, holding her lip with tears welling up in her eyes. I almost felt sorry for her for a split second, but she really had us fucked up.

Grabbing Trevin's head, Paige started kissing all over him, then ran her tongue up and down his cheek. "What you gon' do about this? Try it, bitch!"

Trevin didn't seem fazed, which was hilarious. I chuckled as Kim got up and tried to help her friend with the now spaghetti noodle legs up.

"I can't believe you, Trevin! I can't even believe that this is how things turned out between us. One thing I do know, though, is that I'm definitely putting your ass on child support."

"Or maybe I should just get full custody because what job do you have? At almost thirty-seven years old, you don't have shit but good pussy, so again, what job do you have, huh? What income do you have? That insurance money you got when your mom died isn't going to hold you over forever! I'm sure you ran through that shit already." Trevin sucked his teeth and waved her off. "Fuck out of here."

"Okay, so? I might not have income coming in, but at the same time, I know damn well that a judge would not give the kids over to you! You're barely ever around. You're always on tour around half-naked hoes, illegal drugs, guns, and who knows what else! They are not giving my kids to you...watch and see."

Kim snatched her friend's hand and practically dragged her away before Trevin could say anything.

"Fuck! Trevin shouted before angrily walking off.

My sister eyed me, and I mouthed for her to go after him. Although she didn't know him that well, I could tell she had a thing for him. They had been vibing all day together, so it was only right that she went to check on him and make sure he was good. The second she walked off, I, on the other hand, went over to my car and opened the door.

I was beyond tired, and the first thing I was going to do was snatch off those heels. I sat in the driver's seat, took the shoes off, and threw them into the back seat. Just as I was about to close the door, Assad appeared out of nowhere and grabbed my door before it closed.

"You good?" he quizzed.

I nodded with a smirk. "Yes, but is the next three weeks going to be like this? You got a bunch of bitches I gotta slump or what?"

He chuckled. "I ain't gon' lie, shawty, I never seen no shit like that before."

I laughed as well. "I bet you haven't. Based upon that whole interaction with Kim and her little friend whom you obviously had something going on with, it seems like you only like the type of women who hold their hand out for some money. The type who can't fight worth a damn."

"Nah, that's not true at all, but at the same time, I'm not asking them if they know how to fight before they fuck with me. Hell, maybe I should after tonight."

I lifted my foot up to massage it. They were throbbing like crazy, and I just wanted to shower and lay it on down for the rest of the night. Surprisingly, Assad kneeled and grabbed my foot.

"Maybe you should. And what are you doing?" My brows rose as we silently stared into each other's eyes.

"What the fuck it look like, mama?" I was about to say something to his slick ass, but a moan came out instead when he started showing my pinky toe some love.

I quickly placed my hand over my mouth, and he smirked. "Nah, let that shit out."

I playfully hit his shoulder. "Boy, shut up."

"You mean, man, 'cause ain't shit over here little. A boy could never do the things I do."

I fought the urge to ask him to show me and looked away from his fine ass.

"Okay, man... mister sir... you never answered my question. Am I going to be fighting other women for the whole three weeks that I'm with you? If so, we can just call this whole deal off right now, and you can just figure out another way for Izzy to repay you. I don't even feel like having to..."

I shut up when he got close as hell to my face. Somehow, even after being on set all day, his breath was heavenly, and his scent was mesmerizing. My eyes fluttered, thinking this nigga was about to kiss me. I was ready to close my eyes.

"I sincerely apologize about Myra. She and I were never together, and she was out of pocket. I am looking forward to moving you in with me. The shit happened so fast, and this is new to me, but you have my word that I'll never let another woman touch you in my presence."

I couldn't think. I couldn't breathe. I felt like my soul left my body for a second.

"You accept my apology?" he continued.

"Huh? Oh... yeah... yeah, I accept."

Leaning forward, he kissed me on my forehead, and had Paige not come to the car, I would have lost it. I looked away from Assad for a second to look over at my sister as she climbed into the passenger seat and closed the door.

Paige then looked back and forth between the two of us and said, "Oh shit, am I ruining y'all moment or something becauseee... I can get out." She had a wide grin on her face as I playfully rolled my eyes.

"Nope, we were just talking," I quickly said, but I so desperately wanted him to walk away. As a woman in a relationship, how I felt in that moment, lusting for a man I didn't even know, was so out of character for me.

"Looks like more than talking to me." She pointed to my foot still in his hands.

"Bruh, you ready?" Trevin asked as he walked up, wasting no time, and I didn't blame him.

Assad released my foot and stood, nodding but never looking away from me. "I'll come pick you up tomorrow." He turned to leave.

"Wait. What about my car? And you don't even have my address!"

He spun around and started walking backward. "I know more than you think I know, and you won't need your car. Trust me." He winked at me and headed to his car with his brother in tow.

The second I closed my car door and got comfortable, we both said, "Damn! Now those are some fine ass brothers!"

"Jinx, bitch. You owe me a soda." I laughed as I cranked the car.

"Girl, fuck a soda. I'm hungry again. Let's grab some food," my sister said.

"Bet." I had been so occupied with the fight and then Assad massaging my feet that I didn't even realize I was hungry until she mentioned it. "Shit, I could go for some Cook Out and a banana smoothie."

I pulled off with Assad on my mind, lowkey wishing I could fast-forward to tomorrow.

Chapter Nine

DE'ARRA

When I walked into the house, the last thing I expected to see was rose petals on the floor, dinner on the table, and candles. This was the first time Izzy had ever done something like this, so I was very shocked.

I expected to come home, curse his ass out, break my foot off in his ass, go to bed, and then wake up tomorrow and get this thing with Assad over with. Seeing this was for sure taking me aback... like, my mouth was wide the fuck open, and so was the door.

Izzy hopped up from the couch, holding a bouquet of flowers, and walked over to me. He closed the door behind me and locked it before holding his hand out for me.

"Babe, what is this? And why didn't you tell me? I already ate on my way home."

He shook his head. "Baby, it's okay."

I placed my hand into his as he walked me over to the table and sat me down before handing me the flowers.

It was then that I noticed he was playing old-school R&B love songs in the background, which was one of my weaknesses.

"Thank you, but what's going on?"

"Listen, I don't want to fight anymore, and I want you to know that I got a job."

"Wait, what?" I shouted so loud I was sure the neighbors heard me through the thin ass walls. 'Job' wasn't even in this nigga's vocabulary.

Izzy chuckled. "Yes, I got a job for you... well, for us. You're right about the way things have been going, and I wanted to change that. It doesn't pay that much, but it's a start."

I laid the flowers on the table and hopped up to hug him. "Oh, my God, baby! That's amazing. What will you be doing?"

"Well, nothing major, but I got a job doing security."

"Okay, well, I'm very proud of you." I had been gone from the house all day and really wanted to take a shower. Pointing down at my clothing, I said, "Well, just give me a minute to freshen up, and then we can—"

"Or..." He cut me off midsentence with a kiss. "We can shower together."

* * *

"Oh, fuck, Izzy."

I was bent over in the shower with my hands on the side of the tub as he pounded my shit from the back. All that could be heard was the sounds of the shower as well as the smacking of our bodies against one another as he gave me long, hard, deep strokes.

The truth of the matter was that I was thinking about Assad and how fine he was. He was so damn mysterious, handsome, and rich. Everything about him made my pussy jump all day while I was around him. I couldn't wait to see him tomorrow, and he was for sure on my mind the whole I was having sex with Izzy.

Izzy slapped my ass, making it sound off in the bathroom with a loud echo. My cheeks were now stinging, but in a good way. He was giving it to me so damn good and so hard that my hands were slipping, and I almost lost my footing.

"Damn, bae, you ain't never been this wet before."

I secretly rolled my eyes because this wetness wasn't for him. Although he was fucking me good, I just felt it in my soul that Assad could fuck me ten times better.

Girl, you're tripping. Why are you thinking about having sex with Assad? You have a man! You need stop thinking about Assad!

Shaking away my inner thoughts, I proceeded to fix my footing by spreading my legs a little wider, and then I began to throw it back like there was no tomorrow. When I looked over my shoulder, Izzy's mouth was wide open, and his eyes were practically at the top of his head.

"Ima fuck around and nut in you, bae, damn... Ahhh!" he said when I clenched my pussy muscles around his dick, all while speeding up.

I felt my nut coming as well, so he grabbed my waist, holding on tightly and fucking me back. It was like we were having a fucking match, both of us trying so hard not to lose.

"Cum on this dick, baby."

"I'm cuming, daddy."

A few pumps later, I came on his dick, and then a few moments later, he quickly pulled out of me and nutted in the shower. We were both breathing heavily as I stood and turned around to face him.

"Thank you, baby, for finally putting me first." I kissed him as he smiled widely.

"Thank you for loving me the way you do. I don't know what I'd do without you."

IZZY

After fucking De'arra's gullible ass to sleep, I hopped up, careful not to wake her, and headed for the bathroom to freshen up.

I told her I had a job because I didn't feel like hearing her bitch 24/7 about the shit. I was a street nigga; in fact, the streets raised me, and I was never leaving. With the dick I had just put on her, I knew that even if she did roll over in the middle of the night, she wouldn't be pissed about me not being next to her. I had the shit all planned out.

She thought I had a security job, so if anything, I'd tell her ass that I had to work and thought I mentioned it to her. I went as far as to have my homeboy order an extra uniform from his job and give that shit to me.

De'arra had my heart for sure, but there were some things we always butted heads about, and that was the streets and money. Personally, I loved having my bitch take care of me like the king I was. So much so that I had a whole different bitch named Kim giving me money and buying me expensive ass shit that I kept at her crib. She got her money from her rapper baby daddy, who she had two kids with.

See, De'arra thought a nigga didn't have money, and my clothes definitely reflected that when I was around her, but any time I was in the streets, I was fresh from head to toe while my jewelry blinded niggas. I drove the flyest cars, yet De'arra knew nothing about my second life. I had different women all around the city who were so damn in love with a nigga that they didn't mind me keeping my shit over at their places.

Slanging good dick came with its perks because Kim, my personal ATM, funded my flashy lifestyle, and all I ever gave her ass was dick and bubble gum. She didn't even care that I had a girl at home. She was the perfect sugar mama if you asked me.

All in all, I was going to love not having De'arra sweating me for three whole weeks. I wasn't even worried about her fucking off on me, either. She loved the fuck out of a nigga and would never give my pussy away.

"Took you long enough to get here." Kim left the door unlocked for me, so when I made it into the house, she was sitting on the couch pouting.

"You know I had to wait until my girl was sleep and... wait... the fuck happened to your face?"

She gave me a side-eye. "I don't even wanna talk about it."

"No, tell me what the fuck is going on, Kim."

Yes, I used her for money, and she used me for good dick, but along the way, we did catch a little bit of feelings for each other. Unlike my homie Millz, who was dating De'arra's sister, I would never put my hands on a woman. I tried to stay out of their business as much as I could, but despite what De'arra thought, I always let Millz know that hitting Paige was uncalled for. That nigga had a mind of his own, though, and I wasn't tryna go back and forth with him about some shit that wasn't my business to begin with. So, I stopped putting my two cents in.

As far as Kim, she and I had been messing around for about two years. She never nagged me, got on my nerves, or tripped about me being in the streets or anything like that. She was actually quite happy to have me around because she was dealing with the on-and-off situation with her baby daddy.

He, according to Kim, got a little fame, got a little money, and started acting funny with her after they had their second child. So, she just missed having a man around the house, even if that meant she had to pay me for my time.

See, Kim was a little older than me. I was thirty-one, and she was almost thirty-seven, but she kept that on the hush when it came to the public and the blogs knowing. She was badder than a toddler, so you couldn't tell even if you looked at her face with a damn magnifying glass since black don't crack. Either way, it didn't make me no never mind as long as I got my money, and she kept throwing that pussy at me.

She sighed. "I popped up on my baby daddy, and he had some woman with him. They were all up on each other when I walked in. And then ol' girl had her sister with her, so we all got into it. Me, her, her sister, and Myra. It was a mess."

"Want me to grab some ice for you?" I was glad to hear that it wasn't her baby daddy who put his hands on her.

She shook her head. "No, it's cool. I already put some ice on it when I first got home. I'll make sure to ice it again before I go to bed."

"Aight, cool." I nodded before flopping down on the couch next to her. She then leaned over on the side of me and reached under a pillow. She pulled out a wad of cash and handed it to me with a big smile on her face. "Here's what you came for. And now..." she reached into my pants, "pull that dick out."

"Yes, ma'am." I complied as she pulled up her dress before straddling me.

My dick sprang out of my boxers, and her mouth watered at the sight of it.

"I haven't seen you in a few days. I sure did miss that dick."

I wrapped my arm around her back, lifting her lil ass up so I could use my free hand to put my dick inside her.

"Show me then."

Chapter Ten

PAIGE

"Can you please talk to me?" Millz said when I walked into my home. I rolled my eyes and marched right up to him with my hand out.

"What?" He quizzed, confusedly.

"You need to give me my key back because, as I stated to you yesterday, you and I are completely done. The fact that you have the audacity to even show up here, knowing that you got your ex pregnant for the second time, is pretty crazy to me. I want nothing to do with you. I don't wanna see you, be with you, be around you, nothing! Give me my fucking key back and get the fuck on before I call the police on your no-good, cheating, two-timing ass."

"Yo, who the fuck is you talking to like that, Paige? I'll beat yo'... AHHH!"

I pepper sprayed his ass, then kneed him in the balls. He fell to the floor, crying out for help as I dug into his pocket and grabbed my key. I knew he wasn't smart enough to get a copy made, so I wasn't worried about that.

"My eyes... Bitch, when I—"

"When you what? Huh?"

I pulled out my phone to dial 911, only to see that I had somehow accidentally dialed Trevin's phone number, and the call had been going for two whole minutes. After the fight with Kim and her flunky, Trevin stormed off. I helped calm him down a little, and we exchanged numbers before De'arra and I left. This was not how I expected our first phone convo to go.

"Shit," I mumbled before putting the phone to my ear. "H-hello?"

"Paige? What the fuck is going on?" Trevin asked, concern evident in his voice.

"I'm so sorry. I must have dialed you on accident. Everything is good over here, I promise."

"Nah, everything doesn't sound good. Shoot me your addy right quick."

"I promise you everything is okay. My boyfriend... I mean, my now ex-boyfriend, who was sleeping with his baby mama and got her pregnant again, came over here to start some shit with me. I pepper-sprayed him, and now he's on the floor, crawling around like a little bitch with his eyes burning. Trust me, I got everything under control."

"I understand that, mama, but I would feel better if you sent me the addy. I just got dropped off at my crib. It's nothing to hop in my car and make sure you're straight."

I sighed. "Okay. I guess that's fine."

I watched Millz squirm on the ground and kicked his ass. "Shut the fuck up with all that yelling and shit!" I shouted at him before pulling the phone from my ear and tapping on Trevin's name.

"Aight, I sent you my location."

"Bet. Say less." We ended the call as Millz felt around on the ground, trying to make it to the bathroom to rinse his eyes as if that was going to help.

I sat on the couch unfazed because I knew Trevin was on his way. Millz's scrawny ass was no match for Trevin or my pepper spray, which would be burning his eyes for at least a good twenty to thirty minutes.

If I could kick my own ass, I would because all the times he put his hands on me, I just took it and fought back as much as I could. To see him squirming like a little bitch from a little pepper spray was priceless. I should have been pepper sprayed this nigga.

* * *

"You okay?" I went from seeing Trevin on social media, in blogs, on TV, and all of that to now seeing him twice in one day. Him being at my home was literally surreal, even after spending the whole day with him and kissing those pillow-soft lips of his. "Paige?"

"Huh? Oh... he's uh... in the bathroom still, so I'm good."

"Bet. Say less. Point me in the direction of the bathroom."

I nodded before turning and putting on my stank walk, knowing he was probably looking at this juicy booty. I wasn't ashamed to say that his big, strong ass being there to reprimand Millz was making my pussy sopping wet.

"He's in here." I took Trevin into my bedroom.

Giving it a once over, I was glad I had cleaned up before leaving the house and actually made my bed because that was something I rarely did. I was always in such a rush when heading to the shop to make sure I was never late meeting my clients. So, a lot of times, my room looked like a tornado had hit it. Of course, Millz didn't care to clean up. He typically left that up to me.

My eyes grew wide when I saw Trevin pull out his gun, but I remained calm.

"Lead the way."

Millz had the water running in the bathroom sink and his face underneath the running water. I stepped into the bathroom first and tapped Millz on the shoulder.

With his eyes still closed, he said, "Bitch, don't fucking touch me. On my mama, when my eyes stop burning, I'm fucking you up!"

Trevin gave me the signal to step to the side, so I did. He then placed his gun to Millz's head and said, "You think putting your hands on a woman is a fucking accomplishment, fuck nigga? Stand up straight and say that shit again with me standing right here. I dare you to."

After hearing a deep voice and feeling the gun at the back of his head, Millz froze in place, slowly standing up. We were both standing behind him, so he squinted his now bloody red eyes as much as he could and looked in the mirror, making eye contact with Trevin.

"Paige, what in the fuck do you have going on?" His mouth was lowkey trembling, but he tried to hold it together.

"Say that shit to me, nigga! I'm the one with a fucking gun to your head."

"With all due respect, homie, this ain't got shit to do with you and has everything to do with me and my woman. Paige is my bitch, so w-whatever the fuck you had going on with her, that shit is d-dead, my nigga!"

Hearing Millz stutter made me smirk just a little because that meant Trevin was absolutely succeeding in putting fear in his heart. This was what happened when you walked around like you were untouchable. Trevin was showing Millz that he wasn't untouchable, not even a little.

I wasn't expecting Trevin to pistol whip Millz, but he did, causing him to fall to the ground with a gash on his head as he leaked blood onto my white tiled floor. He moaned and groaned as Trevin got down to his level.

"This woman right here doesn't deserve you putting your hands on her, and this better be my first and fucking last time coming over here and telling you this shit. Whether Paige chooses to keep fucking with you or not is none of my business, but like I just said, don't put your hands on her again. Next time, it's a bullet in your head nigga. You understand?"

Millz nodded the best he could as Trevin yanked him up off the ground like he was a rag doll. I had to put my hand over my mouth to hide my smirk that had now turned into a smile. "That's what the fuck I thought. Now, bring your ass on. The lady already told you to leave, so that's exactly what you're about to do."

He practically dragged Millz to the door and threw him out like Uncle Phil used to throw Jazz out. The shit was comical the way Trevin straight tossed that nigga, and I couldn't wait to tell De'arra.

* * *

"Make sure you wash that cup when you're done with your booty-eating ass," I kidded with Trevin, who was sitting on my couch, enjoying some leftover spaghetti I'd cooked the other day. He was fucking it up and was on his second plate, so I gave him some lemonade to wash it down. "Matter of fact, just take the cup with you. Ain't no telling where Kim's bootyhole done been."

Trevin choked on his food, dying from laughter. "You can believe that silly ass girl if you want to. I ain't eat her ass the other day, last week, last month, or ever. I'm not saying I don't eat ass, but I damn sure ain't eating hers."

Although De'arra and I had already eaten, my greedy ass still fixed a small plate of spaghetti for myself. I smacked my lips before taking a bite of my food. "Mhm. Tell me anything."

"It's the truth, mama. A nigga ain't got a reason to lie to yo' pretty ass."

For the past hour, my lips had been hurting from smiling so much. Trevin was funny and such a sweetheart.

"Well, I appreciate the honesty because, after that kiss we shared earlier, I was lowkey feeling a way since ol' girl said you were munching on her ass."

"Not munching on her ass." He chuckled, setting his plate down on the table. "You're funny. I like that."

"Well, I like that you like that."

Licking those succulent lips again, he smirked. "Stop flirting with me, shawty. This ain't what you want."

Tilting my head to the side, I narrowed my eyes at him. "Maybe I'm not flirting with you. Just maybe, you secretly want me to be flirting with you, but uh…" I set my plate down and then sat back on the couch, getting comfortable. "We're just having a conversation, and there's no harm in that, right?"

We silently stared at each other, but the attraction was there, and it felt like unseen forces were magnetically pulling our bodies together. Before I knew it, I was all over him, and his tongue was down my throat.

Chapter Eleven

DE'ARRA

"Bitch, wait. So, Trevin came over, pistol whipped Millz after you pepper sprayed him, threw him out, y'all ate, kissed, and didn't fuck?"

"That's what I said, ain't it?" Paige tried to suck her teeth and catch an attitude, all because I asked her if she fucked Trevin.

If she did, I wouldn't be mad at her because Trevin really came through in the clutch by coming over and handling Millz like the fuck nigga he was. I wish I could have been a fly on the wall to see him lying on the floor with bloodshot eyes from Paige pepper spraying him and a gash in his head from being pistol whipped.

"Baby girl, don't get your thong in a bunch. If you fucked that man, then you fucked that man. It is what it is."

She shot me the bird before handing me my old faithful curling iron that had gotten me through a lot of shit. Our nana got us a matching pair way back when we first decided we wanted to do hair. I missed Nana like crazy, but at least I knew she was no longer in pain.

Paige and I were currently at my spot, packing up three weeks' worth of clothes and shoes for when I went over to Assad's crib. A smile graced my face just thinking about seeing him, which was crazy. I wasn't even this giddy about my own nigga.

"Girl, bye. We kissed, and that was it, but girl... I swear I'm in love." She playfully and dramatically fell back on my bed. I rolled my eyes and continued to pack as she quickly hopped up. "Wait... I saw rose petals in the living room. Y'all probably was in here fucking and ain't even much changed the sheets."

I laughed. "Sounds like you should have been a detective instead of a hair stylist, sis."

She made a disgusted face. "Ehh... now I gotta take like six showers today." Paige then opted to sit at my computer desk instead.

I looked at the time and started moving a little faster. I overslept and woke up to a text from an unknown number that said, *Good morning, beautiful. I'll send a ride for you around 11 a.m. Can't wait to have you to myself.*

I used the process of elimination and realized it was Assad texting me. Even with crust in my eyes and my breath on ten, I smiled widely at that, then hopped up to get ready.

"And I guess since you gave him some nookie, you didn't press him about that big fat fib his slow ass told." She shook her head. "As if you wouldn't find out."

"Big fat fib?" I burst out laughing, but Paige didn't laugh. She was dead serious, which made me laugh harder. "Please don't say that shit again, and no. It's kind of hard to confront someone when you're getting dicked down really good." I paused, looked up from my bag, and then over at my sister. "My neck is killing me... hell, my back too." I placed my hand on my neck and massaged it a little.

She shook her head. "Ugh... he did not deserve pussy, De'arra."

"Yeah, well, it's too late. Plus, does it count if I was thinking about Assad the whole time?"

Paige's mouth dropped wide open. "Bitch, what? You got me over here feeling bad for making out with Trevin last night when you were fucking your nigga and thinking about the next nigga at the same time! Bitch, you're trifling! No, actually, you're a scandalous hoe!"

"Bitch, shut up." I threw a sock at her. "Yo' ass needs to lay off the urban romance novels 'cause that's exactly what the hell you sound like."

Hopping up and placing her hands on her hips, Paige continued. "Don't change the subject. How did that even happen?"

"I don't knowww," I whined. "Honestly, he was just on my mind heavily after we left the auditions. I was thinking about the way he was massaging my feet with those massive hands. Or maybe it was the way he walked with his legs wide like he was toting a third leg in his pants. Mmm... or his deep ass, sultry, baritone voice that keeps ringing in my ears, captivating my soul and my pussy at the same time!" I fanned myself as Paige did the same, mimicking me.

"Sounds like we got it bad for them fine ass Lattimore brothers. Whew!"

"You could say that again." I zipped my bag—well, one of my bags, and set it by my room door with the other bags.

"So, what are you going to do about Izzy? I mean, he did tell you that Assad was going to kill him. I heard some rumors about both Assad and Trevin, but after yesterday, I think it was all just he say, she say. Now, I'm not saying them niggas ain't got shooters 'cause I'm sure they do, but... Izzy was making it seem like he was literally a dead man walking."

"Honestly, I don't know." I grabbed another bag, which mainly held my shoes, and zipped it up. "I may just let that shit slide because I feel we're finally in a good space. Last night, he got me flowers, made dinner, and had candles lit because he got a job and wanted to surprise me."

"Okay, as I've said a million times, I know I'm not the best person to give advice... yes, we know that. However, I personally don't feel like he should have been rewarded with pussy or anything at all, for that matter, just because he finally got a job. That's something he is supposed to do to help provide for you. Hell, to help provide for himself! He's been mooching off you for as long as I can remember. What kind of job did he get anyway? Is it even paying good, and does it have benefits?"

I shrugged. "I don't know. I didn't ask him all of that, but he said it's a security job, and quite frankly, I don't even feel like having this conversation right now. He said he's going to help out with the bills, and that's all I've been asking him to do. He said he's also leaving the streets alone, and I believe him."

Paige sucked her teeth. "Okay, I'll drop the conversation, lil' sis, but just know Mama ain't raise no fools, so don't be one for this nigga."

"I got it. I got it."

"Y'all talking about me?" In walked Izzy with a smirk on his face as he came over and kissed my cheek.

"Actually, we were, nigga. I hear you got a lil' job or whatever. You must have realized that my sister was about to leave your broke ass, huh?"

"Don't you have somewhere to be? I could have sworn you had an appointment with Millz's fist," Izzy countered, making my mouth drop.

He and my sister always had a lot of back-and-forth bickering going on, kind of like Martin and Pam, but he had never said anything out of the way like that before. He must have fallen and bumped his God damn head talking to my sister any kind of way in front of me like I wasn't gonna stand up for her.

With my hand on my hip and my other finger pointed in his face, I said, "Nigga, don't you ever disrespect my sister like that. Are you fucking crazy? No real man would ever put his hands to a woman's face, and for you to joke about that shit like its nothing… you really just landed yourself in the doghouse even more than you already fucking were."

"Man, I ain't even tryna hear none of this shit. Fuck it, I'm out. I guess I'll see you in three weeks." He darted out of the room just as quickly as he had come.

Izzy… Izzy!" I shouted his name, but he kept walking as if he didn't hear me.

"Girl, fuck him!"

* * *

"Thank you so much," I said to the white male dressed like a penguin. He was older and had hair on the sides but none on the top of his head. He smiled as he grabbed my bags with myself and Paige's nosy ass in tow.

"I so envy you right now, sis."

The guy, who didn't speak or say much of anything, put my bags in the front trunk of the Tesla and then opened my door for me. What I did not expect was for Assad to be sitting inside with a wide smile on his face.

"Good morning, ladies. I hope all is well since yesterday."

I looked at Paige and smirked because a lot of shit had taken place between then and now. In fact, I was sure he already knew about his brother pistol whipping Millz but was being modest.

"Yes, we're good, and you better not try no shit with my little sister, or I'm on yo' ass like a bloody pad. Hence, I said 'bloody' for a reason."

I burst out laughing, and so did Assad as he threw his hands up in mock surrender. "I won't, Mama. You got my word on that."

"Mhm." She smacked her lips. "We will see." Paige gave me a hug and kissed my cheek.

"Love you, sis, be safe." She then whispered, "Enjoy your time off from work and this rich ass nigga at the same time. Don't let Izzy be the reason you don't enjoy yourself."

IZZY

"Nigga, you look like shit," I said when I pulled up on Millz, who was at his mama's crib for whatever reason.

"Ishmael, you know better than to curse in my mother fucking house. Now, show me some respect," Millz's mother said as I laughed and walked up to her, giving her a hug and a kiss.

"How you go tell me not to curse then curse in the same sentence?"

"This my shit, lil' nigga."

I shook my head as she walked off, mumbling something. As soon as she was out of earshot, I repeated myself. "Nigga, you look like shit. The fuck happened to you?"

"That bitch Paige pepper sprayed me, then she had some nigga pistol whip me."

Paige was feisty but not as feisty as De'arra, especially when it came to Millz. Over the past few years, I had lost count of how many times he beat on her, and De'arra had to go rescue her. For Paige to have pepper sprayed him, she must've been completely fed up and done with his ass.

"Pistol whipped by who?"

He sucked his teeth before lighting his blunt. "Hell if I know, but fuck Paige and that nigga."

I burst out laughing. "Wait, you leaving Paige alone just like that? Don't tell me that nigga done put some fear in your heart and shit."

Millz pulled from his blunt and gave me a death glare. "Don't fucking play with me. I fear no nigga. I'm just not interested in continuing a relationship with her dumb ass."

You're the one who looks dumb as fuck.

My brows rose. He was for sure lying and talking out the side of his neck. Just as much as De'arra was my bitch, Paige was his. I had never heard him talk like that, so he was clearly not telling me the full sorry about what the fuck went down.

"Yeah, aight."

I shook my head, grabbed my phone from my pocket, and began to scroll through Instagram as his mother poked her head into the living room.

"You want something to eat, baby? A sandwich or something?"

"No, I'm good, Mama. Thank you." I gave her a small smile.

I had known this nigga for about six or seven years now, so his mama was like my mama. Ms. Jeanie was cool as fuck and didn't care what you did at her house as long as the police didn't come knocking. She also babied Millz's ass, so it was no wonder that he was back on her couch after whatever happened with him and Paige.

"No problem, suga. I'll bring you a sandwich, Maynard. I already know what my baby likes."

"Thanks, Ma," he chimed before passing me the blunt.

Ms. Jeanie turned to walk away, and my phone fell off my lap when I tried to sit back and get comfortable. I wasn't paying attention to what was on the screen at first until I picked it up and saw De'arra in a bikini, lying pool side while some buff nigga served her drinks. The caption said, *Moving on to bigger and better things.*

"You good, bruh?" Millz asked, pulling me away from my phone for a second.

"Look at this shit."

I passed Millz my phone. "Damn. I knew De'arra had a body on her, but shit! That's what the fuck she chose to wear while she's at that nigga's crib?" Millz knew all about the situation and how I finessed both De'arra and Assad. I pulled from the blunt as he passed my phone back. "The fuck you gon' do, nigga?"

I shrugged. "Nothing but double tap that motherfucker."

"I don't know, man. I know you said that the purpose of this shit was to help pay off that 100k you owe Assad. However, he got money, fame, a nice ass car, a nice ass crib, and all that shit. This might backfire on your ass, honestly."

"Are you forgetting that I got money, cars, and all that shit, too? She ain't going anywhere. I'm far from worried."

"Nah, are you forgetting that De'arra doesn't know you're living a whole double life in these streets? You just might get yo' bitch stolen by a pretty nigga. Once she gets a whiff of living lavish, what makes you think she still gon' wanna fuck with you and continue living in the hood at that?" He chuckled as I cut my eyes at him. "Like, what are you going to do? Pop out with all your money, cars, and jewelry, and tell her you won the lottery or some shit?"

This was the shit I hated about Millz, although he was my boy. We both made fast money. However, he was always spending his money on dumb shit like bitches in the strip club, drugs, the several baby mamas he had that neither Paige nor Marjorie knew about, bad investments, and he got swindled out of money for pyramid schemes a few times. The nigga was just slow.

"Nigga, shut the fuck up and worry about that gash buddy put in your head and how you got two new babies on the way. What is that now? Six kids?"

He rolled his eyes, and we smoked silently while his words lowkey started to get to me.

Chapter Twelve

DE'ARRA

"Thank you so much."

Living with Assad was going to be a breeze. After a quick tour of his house and him laying down some ground rules, it was a piece of cake. He asked me not to be too loud if he was working and mentioned that he didn't want me to invite everybody and their mama over to his crib because he didn't want everybody to know where he stayed.

However, I let him know the only person I really fucked with was my sister, so if anything, she would be the only one visiting.

After putting away my things, I threw on a sexy ass yellow bikini that left little to the imagination, grabbed a towel, then headed for the pool. He had some guy there making drinks and literally serving them to me. I didn't catch the guy's name, but he was an older black guy who didn't say much other than when he asked what I wanted.

I was on my second Long Island and tipsy for sure halfway through the drink, so I made sure to put that shit down and pace myself. I didn't wanna overdo it and throw up in this man's pool.

I snapped a few pictures after placing my phone on the tripod I'd brought with me. I mainly used it for my clients, but given the situation, it came in handy. As soon as I posted a few pics, my DMs were flooded with all kinds of smiley faces and heart eyes.

I looked damn good, and there was no reason not to share it with the world.

"You having fun?" Assad startled me.

"Yeah, I'm actually about to... oh, my God." This man's skin was glistening and shit. His hair was now messy and loose. Then he had the nerve to smile at me.

"You good, mama?" He chuckled. "Need some water? I see you out here throwing these drinks back."

"Yeah... Sorry, I uh... I was about to say that I'm about to get in the pool."

"Good, because I don't want to swim alone." He held out his hand to help me, and of course, I dropped my phone off my lap when I got up. I bent down to grab it, and all I heard was, "Damn," which caused me to smirk.

After I placed my phone on the chair, we made our way over to the pool. I dipped my foot inside, only to discover that the temperature was just right.

* * *

After about thirty minutes of swimming and learning a few new things about each other, Trevin showed up.

"I see you looking around," I teased. "No, my sister isn't here, but she can be. All you have to do is say the word."

It was so cute that I actually saw his ass blush. All I knew was whether my sister told the truth about sleeping with him or not, something clearly happened, and he definitely had it bad for her.

Pulling out his phone, he said, "Or, I can text her directly and tell her to pull up."

I grinned, and even though I was in the water, I placed my hand on my hip. "Oh, my bad. Excuse the hell out of me. Please don't put a gash on my head next."

Trevin shook his head as Assad looked at him, confused. "I know damn well you ain't get into a fight and didn't tell me, your manager, about it." I could hear the slight aggravation in his voice, and his face said it all.

"Chill, bruh, it's handled. I don't wanna tell Paige's business and shit, but just know I handled what needed to be handled for her last night."

"Aight, bet. We're vibing today, so I ain't gon' light yo' ass up in front of company, but we will talk about this shit, nigga. I can't have my artist getting into random fights. I told you this already."

They silently stared at each other for a few moments, so I splashed Assad with the water to ease some tension.

He looked over at me, and instantly, his demeanor changed. "Aight now, if I splash your pretty ass back, don't get mad.

"I'm up for a challenge, and did you forget I'm a whole hair stylist? I ain't worried about a little water, baby. It's not like I'm sporting a thirty-inch buss down. I got a whole Nia Long short cut going on." I winked at him, but he surprised me when he started heading my way.

I didn't back down, though, and before I knew it, he was standing right up on me with our faces dangerously close. "Call me baby again and see what the fuck happens."

"Oh, that's what you like?" I challenged him. I didn't see an issue with a little innocent flirting.

"Yes, but since we're on the subject of things I like, I might as well tell you that I like you."

I smiled as he placed his hands under my arms.

"You don't even know me, Mr. Lattimore, so stop trying to run game on me."

"Oh, I'm not, and like I told you before...." He quickly lifted me into the air, startling me. "By the end of all this shit, we will know each other very well. You can count on it."

"Wait, wait, wait.... don't...."

Splash!

He tossed my lil ass into the air, throwing me closer toward the middle of the pool. See, niggas played too damn much. I told him he could splash me with the pool water, not throw me into the deeper end. I couldn't swim worth a damn.

I went under the water and kept coming up, flailing my arms all over the place. I couldn't see or hear much of anything other than the water sloshing. Water was going up my nose really bad and in my damn mouth as I continued to flail my arms.

Bitch, you're about to die.

After what felt like an eternity, I felt a pair of hands around my waist before I was lifted into the air. I started coughing and gasping for air, trying my hardest to catch my breath.

When we finally got to the stairs of the pool, Assad sat me down with a worried look on his face. "I'm so sorry." He patted me on the back. "I had no idea you didn't know how to swim. I would have never done that had I known, mama, I swear to God."

"Yo, is she good, bruh?" Trevin asked from behind me.

I could barely see his face, and I couldn't stop coughing, so I answered him the best I could between coughs.

"It's... okay. I'm...okay."

"Aye, pass me that towel right there."

I assumed he was talking to Trevin. A few moments later, Assad wrapped a towel around me and lifted me bridal style as if I were a feather.

Once we got inside, he took me to the kitchen and sat me on a stool. "Uh... shit. I don't know what to do. Do you need some water or something?"

By now, my coughing had simmered down as I used the towel to wipe my face.

"I need some tissue, please."

"Okay, mama, I got you." He ran off, causing me to chuckle the best I could. Although I damn near died, I knew he didn't do it intentionally, and the concern on his face was rather cute.

"Baby, where are you?" I heard the voice of a woman, which caused me to quickly look in the opposite direction. His kitchen had two entryways, and what I wasn't expecting was to see a woman half-dressed. No, scratch that. The bitch was practically naked with only pasties over her titties and a thong.

Assad ran back into the kitchen just in time, and now the three of us were looking back and forth between each other.

"Yo, Faylen, what in the actual fuck?"

"I just called your sister, and she's on the... Faylen? What the fuck?" Trevin said, and now it was the four of us all looking at each other.

"Oops, my bad. I didn't know you were having company over. All the cars must be parked in the garage, huh?" the Faylen chick said but didn't even bother to cover herself.

"Bi... you didn't know I was having company over because I didn't tell you. Hell, I didn't even invite you, and I just kicked your ass out last night. At this point, you have got to be delusional as fuck to come back in less than twenty-four hours just to get put out again."

He cursed himself for forgetting to change the keypad code.

She ignored him, looked over at me, and then down at the floor, which was now soaking wet. She made a stank face, so I snickered. I might have been wet and just drowned, but a bitch could still get clocked.

"Eww, who is this?"

I stood up from the stool I was sitting on and dropped my towel. I saw her checking out my beautifully sculpted body with envy on her face. "Girl, don't play yourself because *this* has a name, and *this* will mop this wet ass floor with you. Don't play with me, hoe. Play with your mammy!"

She looked shocked, but I didn't care.

"Faylen, take your ass on! You embarrassed the fuck out of my brother. You ain't got no business here. Go back to that lame ass nigga you chose," Trevin said, but Assad intervened.

"Thanks, bruh, but I got it." Assad stepped to Faylen and got very close to her face. "I do not... I repeat... I do not want yo' ass! I just told you this shit last night, and on top of that, this is not the first time we've had this conversation. You turned down my proposal, and there's nothing else for us to talk about! You're married! I don't want to see you, kick it with you, skate with you, or nothing. Get the fuck out, and I will be changing the code!"

He turned to walk away, and she grabbed his arm, whining with her bottom lip poked out. "But, baby, I'm sorry. I love you. I swear I do, and we can fix this... us. I'll leave my husband!"

"Nah, I'm good. See your way out."

The room got really quiet before she charged at me, trying to sneak me. I moved out of the way just in time and slapped fire out of her ass.

"Ahhh!"

"Bitch, you're weak sauce. Pack it up and bounce before you leave here on a stretcher with your shit knocked loose. That man said he don't want you. I'm not your enemy, but I can be, but trust me, you don't want that!"

"Fuck you, hoe! He's just... just... wait, am I bleeding?" She pulled her hand from her lip and saw a lil' speck of blood, nothing major.

"I got this, bruh." Trevin walked over to Faylen and lifted her like a rag doll.

"Hey, put me down!" She started punching him in the back, but Trevin wasn't worried, and I could hear her in the distance saying, "He's only using you to get over me! Trust, I have hard shoes to fill!"

Once silence fell upon us, Assad rushed over to me. "I'm so sorry that happened. Damn, I keep fucking up." He sighed. "Faylen is my ex, but we haven't been together in lord knows how long. I proposed to her in front of all our friends and family, and she turned my proposal down. She moved on, but I guess their shit is rocky since she just started back randomly popping up and reaching out to me."

"Look, it's cool for now, but if this happens a third time, just know I'm beating yo' ass next. And I'm dead ass serious."

Assad chuckled. "Okay... you got it, baby girl."

I picked up the towel that I threw down. "That whole pool fiasco took a lot out of me. I think I'll just shower and lie down."

I turned to walk away and headed for my room while I was staying here.

"I promise it won't happen again!" he said behind my back.

I just kept walking because he was for sure losing brownie points with me.

Chapter Thirteen

PAIGE

"Okay, PooPoo. I'm about to head out. Are you sure you got everything on lock?"

I had just finished cleaning up my area after doing a late install on my last client for the day. My dogs were barking, and my back was aching a little, but I was excited about the fact that Trevin hit me up. He told me he was chilling at Assad's for the day and that I should pull up, so that's exactly what I was about to do. He also said something about my sister almost drowning, which made me laugh just a bit. That bitch couldn't swim and was terrified of going in the deep end ever since we were little kids. I wish I had been there to see that shit.

I did six heads and made some good ass money today, thankfully. It had been a little slow, but after I hired someone to manage our social media page and get as much content as possible, the momentum quickly picked back up. Hoes loved a good, low lace install price. I was doing a 'bring a friend and get $50 off' deal, which kept the shop flooded.

As I reminded PooPoo to set the alarm on her way out and to make sure everything was unplugged, a loud group of women entered the salon.

"Girl, yes, he ain't shit, but I can't leave that nigga alone for real. I love him," one of the ladies stated as I looked at PooPoo, who already knew she needed to handle it. I would curse those hoes out in a millisecond for coming in all loud and rowdy.

"Hey, ladies, and welcome. We're actually closing in ten minutes, but our receptionist can schedule you all for future appointments if you'd like."

"Ten minutes? I really need my hair done, though! I have a red-carpet event to attend, and I need to look good. I'll pay extra." The woman clasped her hands together. Something about her seemed familiar, but she had on huge shades, so I couldn't tell. "See, I even have my wig, and it's already washed and pre-plucked."

PooPoo looked over at me, and I nodded. "Okay, our squeeze in fee is an extra hundred dollars. If you're cool with that, Rose will take your payment, then Sade will get you shampooed."

She clapped her hands and jumped up and down. "Thank you! I just know y'all gon' hook me up. I follow your Instagram, and all them hoes be slayed."

I gave her a fake smile. "Well, thank you. Please see Rose at the window, then have a seat at our shampoo station. By the way, we don't allow extra guests."

She turned to dismiss her flunkies as I turned to text Trevin to let him know I'd be doing one more head before pulling up.

* * *

"Wow, I'm looking like a million bucks," my last minute appointment said, looking in the mirror.

I was glad to finally be officially getting off. The whole salon, including my other stylists, were now gone, so it was just me and ol' girl left.

She handed me back my handheld mirror and stood up to look in the larger full-length mirror we had on the wall. She and I didn't say much of anything to each other the whole time.

Although I was very respectful of my clients, I didn't have much conversation with them. My shop wasn't one of those gossiping ass shops that a lot of women frequented to spread other people's business or anything like that.

When she took off her shades, I wanted to slap that hoe again.

"Wait. I know you didn't have the audacity to come into my shop, sit in my chair, and get your fucking hair did after what the fuck you did yesterday. Are you fucking crazy?"

She laughed. "Girl, that's water under the bridge. Chill out."

"What fucking bridge, and how did you even find me?"

I couldn't believe that Trevin's baby mama really finessed my ass. Now, I was all about making my money, but I would never have willingly done her hair.

She ran her fingers through her thirty-inch platinum blonde wig, spinning around to see it from the back.

"Like I told you, I follow your shop's page on Instagram. This morning, I saw a post and said, 'I just know that ain't the same bitch that's fucking on my baby daddy.'" She looked over her shoulder at me. "I just had to pull up and see for myself."

I scoffed and rolled my eyes. "I'm not fucking your baby daddy, so you came up here for no damn reason."

She snickered, placing her hand over her mouth. "Please pipe down, buttercup. I told you I came to get my hair done. Am I not a paying customer?"

"Girl, get the fuck out. You're doing too much talking right now. Your hair is done. Now go."

Her phone rang, so she answered it with a huge smile on her face. "Hold that thought... hello? Hey, baby daddy. What's up?"

"I cannot believe this shit," I mumbled as I swept up the hair that had fallen to the floor. She had two seconds to get out, or I would bop her in the head with the broom.

"You wanna see my hair?" This bitch called him on FaceTime and started spinning around in a circle, trying too hard to show me in her background.

"Hey, you need to go. I really don't wanna have to ask you again."

"Who's that? Where are you?" Trevin asked.

"Oh, the bitch in the background?" She flipped the camera around and pointed it at me.

"Wait. Is that Paige?" Trevin quizzed. He seemed genuinely confused by what was going on. "The fuck are you doing at her shop?"

Before I knew what came over me, I smacked her phone out of her hands, and it hit the floor hard. I hoped that shit was broken.

"Are you serious right now?" She bent down to pick up her phone, then hollered, "And you cracked my screen!"

Just as I suspected, I couldn't control myself and bopped this bitch in the head with the broom.

Her mouth flew open as Trevin said, "Kim, what the fuck? Why are you always starting shit?"

"Go, bitch!" I shouted at the top of my lungs. "Go!"

"I'm going, but this will not be the last time you see me!"

She snatched up her belongings and scurried away while Trevin chastised her. All I could do was place my face into my hand and take a deep breath. I could not believe this had just happened in real life. This whole shit had just played out like a Tubi movie.

Chapter Fourteen

ASSAD

"You mad at me?" I asked De'arra the second she got out of the shower. She jumped, and I threw my hands up. "I'm sorry, mama. I didn't mean to barge in. I uh... I knocked a few times and thought maybe you were sleeping. I just really wanted to apologize again."

I could kick my own ass for being so rough with her and tossing her lil ass into the deep end without asking if she could swim first. The thought never crossed my mind, and she had a nigga panicking when I saw her arms flailing all around and shit.

"You're good. You definitely scared the shit out of me just now, but you're good."

"That's good to know. Well, if you need anything, don't hesitate to ask. I just want to make sure you're comfortable during your stay.

"Well, other than you trying to kill me, all is well. Your house... it's so beautiful."

De'arra walked over to the bed with her towel on and lifted her leg onto the edge. She then proceeded to lotion her leg, but I looked away since her towel was rising right along with my dick.

"My bad, for real. Let me make it up to you, at least." The room grew quiet, so I looked at her once more, turning to face her.

She stopped what she was doing for a second and looked over at me. "In what way?"

"Honestly, any way that you see fit. I don't like people having a nasty taste in their mouth about me, so whatever you want. Just let me know. Between the pool situation and my stupid ass ex, I just feel like a jackass right now."

"Hmm, so if I wanted you to lay down while I rode your face, would that be a problem?"

She took me aback when she said that because it wasn't something I expected her to say. "Wait, come again? I don't think I heard you correctly."

"I mean, I'm not saying that's what I want. I'm just simply asking a question, Mr. Lattimore." She smirked, and then I knew she was fucking with me.

"You almost had my ass lying flat on the bed for a second. Don't joke like that, 'cause when you get ate the fuck up till you cry, don't say I didn't warn you."

"Mhm... sounds like a threat. Are you threatening me?"

My phone chimed, so I pulled it from my pocket to see that it was the nursing home calling about my grandmother. They had recently changed her meds, and she was acting a little differently, spazzing out on others, disrobing, and all kinds of shit. So, they were always blowing me up to keep me updated.

"One second, beautiful." She nodded as I turned my back to answer the phone.

"Hello?"

"Hey, Mr. Lattimore. Would you mind coming down here in the morning? Ms. Mary Jo has been a little rowdy lately, and she keeps pulling out a picture of you and your brother when you were little. It's been a while since you visited, and if possible, I'm sure she'd love a visit." Nanya, one of my grandmother's nurses, said to me, and I sighed.

I loved her to death, but I hated visiting her because, after her stroke a year ago, she just wasn't the same grandma that we grew up around. She was paralyzed on one side, in a wheelchair, and her speech wasn't as good. She still had her memory for the most part, but I hated seeing her like that. I put her in a home after our grandpa died so she wouldn't be lonely. Since she needed the extra care, it just seemed to make sense.

Hell, I probably hadn't been to see her in about a month. With Trevin popping off with his music and us getting shit together for this movie, time just kind of slipped away, and I felt bad.

"Yeah, I'll stop by in the morning. Thanks for letting me know."

"Of course, Mr. Lattimore. See you soon."

I bid her goodbye, and when I turned back around, De'arra was fully dressed and sitting on the bed.

"Everything good?" Her brows rose as she reached for the remote to turn on the TV.

"Yeah, that was the nursing home calling about my grandma. She had a stroke shortly after my grandpa died last year. They just recently switched up her meds, so I'm going to stop by in the morning and spend some time with her."

"Aww, that's so sweet of you. I'm sure she will be happy to see you."

De'arra gave me a small smile before I sat on the bed next to her.

"Oh, shit." She placed her hand on her stomach. "I am so embarrassed. Did you hear that?"

"Yeah, I heard your stomach. You ain't tell me you were part grizzly bear."

She scoffed. "Ehhh, that was corny, but I'll let you slide for now."

I laughed as I reclined to where I was now leaning on my elbow and on my side, facing her. "Why only for now?"

"Because." She smacked her lips. "I'm more than certain that you'll say something else corny that may top that corny shit you just, so again, for now... I'll let you slide." She winked at me before climbing out of the bed.

My brows rose. "What happened?"

She pointed to her phone. "My sister is here. I'll go let her in."

I hopped up." No, you just relax. I'll have the chef whip up something. What do you have a taste for?"

"Mmm." Her greedy ass closed her eyes for a moment. "Honestly, I'm not picky by a long shot, so surprise me."

"Say less, mama."

I turned to leave, but she said, "Why you always calling me mama? I ain't your damn mama," she teased.

I shrugged before grabbing her chin. "It's just my thing. It's how I talk, but don't act like you don't like the shit. Soon enough, you'll be calling me daddy, so we'll be even."

Her mouth dropped as I left to go let her sister in.

When I got to the front door, I was surprised to see that Paige was outside with my brother, and they were arguing about something. They both stopped when I came outside.

"Y'all good?" I looked back and forth between the two of them, wondering what the fuck they could be arguing about, especially since they just met.

"Yes, and hi, Assad. Please point me in the direction of my sister." She rolled her eyes and then stormed past me into the house.

"Nigga, the fuck you done did now?"

I laughed as he shook his head and sighed. "Man, Kim went to her salon, sat in the chair, and got her whole head done, then started shit with Paige afterward."

"Wait. She ain't recognize Kim from the jump?"

"Nah. She had on some big ass shades, from what Paige told me. But, nigga, that shit was crazy as fuck. I FaceTimed her ass to see my kids, and she turned the camera and shit with Paige in the background. I was confused as fuck."

"Damn," was all I could say because he definitely was on his own with that one.

"Are you coming?" Paige poked her head out the door. "I don't want to just walk around your crib. I have manners, unlike some people."

Trevin threw his hands up. "I can't control the shit my baby mama does."

"You don't have to explain anything to me. I'm not your girl." Paige turned to go back into the house, and I chuckled, placing my hand on his shoulder. "Put Kim in her place, 'cause nigga, if not, she just gon' keep doing the same dumb ass shit."

I went into the house, leaving my brother outside to get himself together. I was glad I didn't have baby mama problems.

PAIGE

"Girl, cut him some slack! Like you said, the two of you are not dating. On top of that, we just met these niggas, so just play it cool. I know he didn't send his dumb ass baby mama up to your shop on purpose, and I can't believe you didn't beat her ass. I would have slapped that hoe across her face with a wand curler so quick. Then I would have snatched the wig off her head. I would have undone the hairstyle that I just did, but maybe that's just me."

My sister had me cracking up as we caught up on the shit that happened to us today. "I know you would have, and girl, you know I wanted to, but I have to be professional. Money is already just a little bit tight, and I don't need to be fucking up all the shit in my salon, fighting the baby mama to a man who isn't even mine."

"I know that's right," she chimed in.

"I'm pretty sure that's what she wanted me to do. I mean, why else would she have taken off those big ass shades at the very end of her hair appointment? She could have easily walked out the door, and I would never have figured out who she was. She was really trying to play in my face and test my patience. Shoot, she probably would have found a way to record the whole thing and post it on social media, too. She seems like that type of bitch."

"Oh, you already know, but it's cool. You did good."

"I just hate that shit is kind of awkward now. I was honestly thinking about his ass all day and how he... you know, manhandled Millz last night. And then the fact that we made out. So, for this shit to happen and for us to start arguing outside not too long ago... I just... I don't know. I have no problem getting to know him, but his baby mama just seems like she isn't going to stop anytime soon. It's the second time she got buck with me over this man."

"Fuck her. At the end of the day, you and Trevin could become the best of friends, or y'all could have a great networking relationship business wise. Or... y'all could be fuck buddies and then possibly end up walking down the aisle. You never know, and you shouldn't allow her to change your mind about that. He seems nice. Honestly, I need to be taking the same advice since I almost knocked Assad's head off when his naked ex popped up in the kitchen. The shit was so random."

"Mhm... let me find out you're team Trevin, and bitch, not his naked ex."

"Girl, yes. And hell, I'm on anyone's team other than Millz. Just go with the flow, sis. You deserve better."

"Thank you."

Knock Knock

"Come in," my sister shouted.

A few moments later, Assad stuck his head through the door. "The food is ready, fat ass. I hope tacos are okay."

"Shut up." De'arra threw a pillow at him. "Don't act like you're not hungry too. And, yes, tacos will do."

"Oh, ain't no shame in my game. A nigga is hungry as shit." We all shared a laugh as my sister stood up to put on her house slippers. "Here, mama, let me help you."

Assad bent down to help her put on her shoes, which caused my sister and I to give each other the eye. In such a short amount of time, Assad and his brother had both shown us different sides of a man that we weren't used to seeing from Izzy or Millz.

"Okay. Y'all cute or whatever."

The second we walked out of the room, I walked right into Trevin, stopping me in my tracks. Assad and De'arra were laughing and talking about something, so they continued to the kitchen. I tried to go around him, but of course, he blocked my way.

"What's up, Trevin?"

"You can call me Tre, and I wanted to chop it up with you right quick."

I scoffed. "Okay, well, Mr. Tre, can't this wait? I'm starving, and the food smells amazing. I could eat a horse right now." I was so busy today with the clients at my shop that I barely had time to stop and eat.

"Hold your horses, hungry hippo."

I playfully punched him in the chest. "Nigga, shut up. I got your hippo!" I jumped up and put him in a headlock. "Say sorry."

Somehow, he actually lifted me in the air, and as a reflex, I wrapped my legs around his waist.

"I'm sorry, beautiful black queen. Now let a nigga go before you make my dick hard."

"Wait, what?" I laughed as he placed me back on my feet after I let him out of the headlock. "I cannot."

I shook my head as he smirked. "I'm just saying, you wrapped them thick ass thighs around me. I ain't know what else to do but get hard."

"Mmm, whatever, nasty. So, what's up?"

I tried to play it off by smoothing my clothes down and avoiding eye contact. His words definitely had me hot and bothered, especially after knowing exactly what his lips felt like two times in one day yesterday.

Whew, lord! Help me!

"I just wanted to say that I don't want there to be any bad blood between us, especially since we'll be working together as scene partners, so I kind of feel like a nigga should apologize for the shit Kim did. It wasn't cool, and I'll handle that. Trust me."

"As you should, and I accept. Now, about this movie. I don't know any details or anything. When is rehearsal, and what days are we shooting?"

He pulled out his phone. "You're right, and I apologize about that. We were interrupted last night before getting your info, but that's on me, mama. My bad."

After providing him my email address to send me the schedule, he said, "Can I tell you something?"

"Yeah, what's wrong?" I glared up at him as he reached for my hand. It was crazy because I didn't know what the hell he wanted to hold my hand for, but I didn't even give a damn. It just felt good to be touched in a loving way.

Bitch, he doesn't love you. He doesn't even know you! How could he be lovingly touching you? Shut up!

I almost wanted to laugh at my thoughts, but I kept a straight face.

"Nothing is wrong. I just had to let you know that I'm feeling you, and I can't get our kiss out of my mind."

All of a sudden, my breath was caught in my throat.

"So, what does that mean?" I couldn't help the wide smile on my face. "Oh, you tryna feel these lips again?"

"If you tryna let me, then hell yeah."

Just as we were about to kiss, all hell broke loose as Assad started shouting. It sounded like shit was either falling or being thrown. I pushed Tre off me and ran fast, trying to make sure De'arra was okay.

Assad was sitting at the dining room table with his hands on his head, and his phone was on the ground with a shattered screen. De'arra stood off to the side with glossy eyes.

"W-what happened, sis?"

She looked past me and over at Tre. "I'm so sorry, Trevin, but... your grandmother had another stroke, and she's being rushed to the h-hospital."

"Oh, my god." I placed my hand on Tre's back as Assad hopped up and stormed off.

"We gotta get to the hospital now," was all he said before the three of us rushed out behind him.

Chapter Fifteen

KIM

"Girl, where is your 'dick for hire' right now?" Myra said, joking about Izzy. We were on FaceTime while I finished cooking dinner for the night.

"Dick for hire? Really, bitch?"

I shook my head and rolled my eyes, not caring if she could see me or not because Myra always said some crazy, off-the-wall shit.

"You know I'm telling the truth. I don't understand why you give most of the money Trevin gives you to his ass. He has money. You see the clothes he wears and the whips he drives. He needs to be giving you money, the fuck. I hate a nigga that's only good for one thing."

"I mean, he doesn't just give me dick. We actually have a good vibe, and he fixed my car when it wouldn't start once. In fact, he's really good with his hands. He's the one who fixed the leak in my bathroom sink. I mean, he doesn't do the shit often, but still... he's cool. And I don't give him all my money. You just saying shit."

I stirred the homemade garlic mash I'd made before taste-testing it.

"Listen, I told you before. It doesn't matter if you give his ass one dollar. It's still supposed to be the other way around. You're the one who laid on your back and made two babies with a popular-ass, rich-ass rapper. Izzy shouldn't be able to reap the benefits of what your pussy did to get you in the position you're in now. That's all I'm saying."

I glared at her through the phone as she sipped her cheap ass wine before I heard the door open. Our situation was definitely different from others, and it wasn't one that I cared to explain to anyone, so I rushed her off the phone.

"Girl, he's here. I'll hit you up later."

"Just think about what I said, and maybe even try to see how he acts if you don't pay him."

I looked over my shoulder to make sure Izzy wasn't near and hadn't heard her. "Girl, bye. I gotta go!"

I ended the FaceTime, and a few seconds later, Izzy rounded the corner.

"What's good, beautiful?" He kissed me on the cheek as I smiled up at him. "Shit, it smells good as hell in here."

Maybe Myra is right. Try and see if he trips if you don't give him money, or even try and see if you can reverse the roles a little.

"Thank you. I made all of this just for you." I smiled as he looked over the feast I'd prepared. I made smothered and fried pork chops with corn, mashed potatoes, and rolls.

"Damn, you made my favorite. You really do be spoiling a nigga."

I popped my imaginary collar. "I try."

"Yeah, I see." He smacked my ass before walking away and heading toward the living room.

"The food is almost done."

"Aight, bet." He sat on the couch and removed his shoes.

After checking on everything, I joined him on the couch. The room grew silent, and I could feel him burning a hole into the side of my face.

"You got something for me, baby?"

I knew he meant money, but with me not knowing where Trevin and I stood, especially after the salon fiasco, I really did need to chill on dishing out unnecessary money.

Paige could have really dragged me all up and down that salon if she wanted to, but one thing was for sure, that bitch slayed the entire fuck out of my hair. I never had my hair this cute before. My wig was definitely giving me scalp.

"You good?" he asked, just as I heard one of my kids crying.

"Yeah, uh... I'll be right back."

I quickly hopped up and headed to the kids' room to find my son, Carmelo, crying his eyes out. I picked him up and patted his back. "Aww, it's okay, baby. What's wrong? Huh? Mommy's baby has a bad..."

My heart stopped as I looked over at my daughter Cassie. She was gasping for air. "No, no, no, no, no!" Quickly putting my son down, I shouted for Izzy. "Izzy! Izzy! Call 911!"

I picked up her clammy body from her crib and flipped her over after seeing a bulge in her throat.

"W-what happened?" Izzy ran in as I started patting my daughter on the back.

I had no idea what I was doing, but I tried my hardest to dislodge whatever she'd swallowed.

"Please just call 911! Something is wrong with my baby!" I was shaking and felt like throwing up. My son continued to cry as Izzy pulled out his phone.

Lord, why is this happening?

Chapter Sixteen

MILLZ

"Oh, I'm trifling? Me?"

"That's what I said, right? What was the reason for you telling Paige that you were pregnant again? I already told you I didn't want another kid, and you're sitting up here trying to force this shit!"

"Nigga, fuck you! You're the one who didn't tell me that you were still with Paige! Like, why would you lie to me and say that y'all broke up and she moved out? Huh?"

My baby mama, Marjorie, had been blowing me up, calling me back-to-back all damn day long, saying we needed to talk in person. So, I told her to pull up on me at my mom's crib.

We were currently in my old bedroom that I had just moved back into. She was yelling, even though I told her dumb ass to stop yelling in my mama's house.

"I never told you no dumb shit like that!"

She burst out laughing. "Oh, so I'm just a crazy ass bitch, pulling all this shit out the crack of my ass, then, huh? You didn't look me in my eyes when you were deep in this pussy and tell me how much you loved me and that you were leaving Paige for me?"

FLEXIN' ON MY EX, LOVING A BOSS

"Man, gone on with all of that. You said you came to talk, not argue. So, if you plan to continue yelling, especially in my fucking mama's house, you can get your dumb ass out. I'm tired as hell and ready to go to bed. I had a long day."

BAM, BAM, BAM!

"Y'all better shut the fuck up in there!" my mama yelled, banging on my room door.

"My bad, Ma. We'll keep it down!" I shouted back through my closed room door.

The truth of the matter was that I did, in fact, say those things to Marjorie. However, I wasn't serious. She and I never worked out in the past, and we damn sure weren't about to work out now. I told her that Paige and I were going through some things and that we were in the process of breaking up. I told her that she was moving out.

I only told Marjorie what she wanted to hear so I could continue smashing. I mean, I knew my soldiers marched, so I really shouldn't have been hitting raw, but we were here now. She wasn't too far along; however, her belly did have a little pudge. I had brought up abortion before, but she was against it.

"No. I'm not going anywhere until you be a man for once and admit that you were playing the both of us! Paige had no idea you were still fucking on me and vice versa, nigga! You're acting like I laid down by myself, and I don't like that. I love yo' ass, but you will not make me out to be the villain. If anything, I'm the victim, not you!"

"Are you done? You getting yourself worked up for nothing. You see where I'm at now, so what the fuck you think that means? Me and Paige not together, so dead that noise and come lay the fuck down."

Just as I suspected, with a frown on her face, Marjorie marched over to the bed and laid her ass up under me.

I wrapped my arm around her, and she looked up into my face. "Why do it have to be like this with us? If you loved me like you say you do, we wouldn't have to keep having the same arguments."

"Bae, just go to sleep. We'll talk in the morning, okay?"

She sighed, getting comfortable. "Okay, fine. I'll drop it for now, but can you just... ahhh! Sorry, I was trying to say that... ahhh!" She sat up, holding onto her stomach.

"What's wrong?" I sat up as well. From the look on her face, I could tell she was in pain.

"I-I don't know. I just got a sharp pain in my pelvic area and... ahh!"

"What's going on? Talk to me."

With tears streaming down her face, she reached between her legs, and we were both surprised to see her hand covered in blood. "I think I'm having a m-miscarriage."

DE'ARRA

"I feel so bad for them. From what Assad told me earlier, they already lost their grandpa, and now this." I sighed, fidgeting with my hands. "I hate hospitals so much. Oh, my God."

"I know, and I feel bad for them too." Paige reached for my hand. "I know hospitals remind you of when we lost Mama. I always blocked out the trauma of seeing her laid up in the hospital bed. All the crying, fake ass family members and their condolences, the whole nine. I know how it makes you feel being here, so do you wanna take a walk?"

I nodded as I felt tears on the brink of falling. "I think I need to just get some fresh air."

"You want me to come with you?" my sister asked.

I nodded, then quickly wiped my tears.

We had been at the hospital for almost two hours, and it was driving me crazy. Plus, we never got to eat, so my head was hurting.

"Let's stop by a vending machine ASAP."

"You read my mind." Paige winked at me as we got up and made our way down the hall.

We chatted about nothing in particular, just to get our minds off the situation at hand. All of a sudden, Paige said, "Okay, umm... how about we split up? I'll go for the snacks, and you go for a walk, but go that way."

She grabbed me by the shoulders, spun me around, and then pointed in the opposite direction of the one we were currently walking in.

My brows rose. "Why? What's wrong?"

"Uh, nothing. I'm just really hungry and would rather grab the snacks now and then come meet you for that walk."

"Girl, no, it's fine. I'll come with you." I spun around, and she dropped her head.

I was confused as hell until I looked up to see my boyfriend with his arms around Kim, of all people. She was crying, and he was consoling her.

"Girl, fuck him and her. Let's just go outside and—"

"You cheating ass, lying ass nigga!" I shouted, which literally made all the staff freeze like a game of freeze tag.

Izzy looked up at me, and I charged at them as Paige held onto my shirt with all her might. But she was no match for me. I was literally a Pitbull in a skirt.

"What the hell are you doing here, and with her of all people?"

Kim quickly hid behind Izzy, which pissed me off even more. "Speak, nigga! 'Cause I'm trying to figure out what my boyfriend is doing at the hospital with another bitch. And while his girlfriend is questioning him about what's going on, he's shielding the bitch from getting knocked the fuck out."

"Chill, bae. It's not even like that. Kim is my homegirl, and she doesn't really have anybody to be here for her right now, so I pulled up."

Bop!

I went across his face with quickness.

"De'arra!" Paige tried to hold me back. "Come on, sis, let's just go."

"No, because he thinks I'm dumb! Never have we ever had friends of the opposite sex. All of a sudden, him and Kim are the best of buddies, to the point that she can call him, and he'll pull up at the hospital to let her cry on his fucking shoulder? Fuck no!"

"Her child choked on a fucking toy and could be dying! Chill out!" Izzy spat, holding the spot on his face that I'd hit.

"The fuck is he talking about?" We all turned to the side to see that Trevin and Assad had walked up.

Trevin obviously caught the tail end of Izzy's sentence, and he was fuming. He stood before us, still like a statue, with his hands balled up, and his face twisted like a pretzel from Auntie Anne's.

"I-I'm so sorry. I don't know w-what happened to Cassie. O-one minute she was okay, and then..." Kim sobbed.

Stepping closer to Kim, Trevin said, "Why the fuck didn't you call me? Where is my baby? Both of them?"

His voice made a few people jump, including myself.

"Bitch!" I heard Paige say.

I looked in her direction to see her now beating the fuck out of Millz's baby mama Marjorie.

What in the actual fuck is going on?

"Paige, stop! Somebody get her!" Millz yelled as security ran over to assist.

With her arms flailing all over the place as security held her in the air, Paige said, "Fuck you! You cheat on me with this bitch, and now you're at the hospital with her?"

Marjorie was lying on the ground as Millz tended to her. I couldn't help but notice the huge gash on his head. Trevin definitely got his ass good.

"She had a fucking miscarriage, and you ain't making shit no better!" Millz said as if his ex having a miscarriage with his baby wasn't an issue.

"Oh, shit!" I placed my hand over my mouth.

"Wooow! So, she was telling the truth. You did get her pregnant again! I hate yo' ass and... put me the fuck down!" Paige managed to escape the security's arms. "You know what, girl? I'm sorry for beating yo' ass, but you can have this abusive, worthless, sorry excuse for a man. Have fun getting beat upside your head, hoe!"

Paige stormed off as security finally spoke up. "Hey, you all need to quiet down or leave the hospital. I'd hate to have to get the authorities involved, but I will."

"No, it's fine. We're so sorry," I quickly said before looking around at everyone's faces.

The security nodded before apprehensively asking Trevin for an autograph.

Through clenched teeth, Trevin looked at ol' boy like he was a rotten egg and replied, "Nigga, do it look like I wanna sign some shit for you right now?"

"My bad. I'll uh... come back another time." The security then scurried away after giving us one last warning.

Millz helped Marjorie up from the ground, but she pushed his hands away and shouted, "Get the hell off me! I'll just Uber home or something. Stay away from me!" She slowly began to walk away as best she could while he followed her, begging for forgiveness.

I placed my hand on Assad's shoulder. "I'm going to go check on my sister."

He nodded, and even though I wanted to stay and be nosey, I definitely needed to make sure my sister was okay. She would have done the same for me.

"The fuck you telling him for? I'm your man!" Izzy shocked me with that statement because he had some nerve.

"I'm not about to do this with you. Besides, he is my man for the next few weeks. That's the way you want it, so that's the way it is. Besides, you have to save space on your shoulder for your *homegirl* to cry on. Excuse me."

I rolled my eyes and walked off in search of Paige.

Chapter Seventeen

KIM

"How could you be so careless, Kim? The fuck were you doing that you weren't watching my children?" He looked directly at Izzy as his jaw clenched along with his fists.

"Oh, don't give me that!" I spat. "I am a mother first, but since I see what you're insinuating... I am a single woman, and I can do as I please. It's not like I left them in the house alone. They were in the room only a few steps away from me."

"I don't give a fuck about none of that. If you can't pay attention to them, being that they are small and need to be watched, then maybe you shouldn't have custody of them!"

I laughed through the tears that wouldn't stop falling. "Like I told you, it was an honest mistake. You are not going to try to make me feel bad about that!"

"First thing in the morning, I'm calling a lawyer, and that's all I'm going to say about it."

"Nigga, fuck you! I hate you!"

Did I really hate him? No. However, he was really pissing me off.

"You don't have them twenty-four-seven, and honestly, this is something that could have happened in your care as well, bruh."

Once Izzy spoke up, all hell broke loose. Trevin charged at Izzy, snatching him up by his collar. "Nigga, who the fuck do you think you are, giving your two cents in a conversation that ain't got shit to do with you?"

"Tre, stop!" I pushed him from behind. "He's right, and you know it!"

"No, the fuck he isn't, and he needs to stay out of another grown man's business."

Tre glared at Izzy, mean-mugging him before throwing his ass backward like a rag doll.

"What the fuck are you doing messing around with this broke ass nigga anyway? He owes my brother 100k, and on top of that, he's in a whole relationship with Paige's sister, De'arra. He pawned her off on my brother to settle his debt."

I knew he had a girl before I started fucking him, so it wasn't news to me. What I didn't know was that he even knew Assad or that he was using his girl to settle his debt. I didn't like Paige's ass or her sister, but Izzy pawning her off wasn't sitting right with me. That was some shit that people only did in movies and books, not in real life. I now knew why De'arra looked so familiar. Her picture was on Izzy's lock screen.

I decided to change the subject. "Izzy, thank you for coming here with me, but I do need to talk to my baby daddy alone."

"Bet. Call me and give me an update on everything."

I nodded before Izzy gave me a hug. On his way out the door, he looked Tre up and down. No cap, it lowkey felt good to see Trevin so mad over Izzy being there. It showed he really did love and care about me, and he was clearly jealous.

"You're clearly jealous of what Izzy and I have." We didn't have shit but sex, and technically, I was his damn sugar mama, but Trevin didn't need to know that.

"Kim, you can't be serious. Our daughter choked, and you're worried about me being jealous? I am so sick and tired of you not prioritizing our children. Like, the shit literally makes me want to snap your neck every time you open your fucking mouth. You say the dumbest shit. I have told you a million times I do not care who you're fucking or sucking. I'm not interested in you. I don't want to be in a relationship with you, and I don't love you in that way. I love you for giving me children, but I'm not in love with you, and you know that. I give you money to make sure you're straight, but I really don't have to. All I have to do is be there for my children, but you're making it hard for me to even want them to be in your care!"

"Whatever. You don't have to admit it, but you're in love with me. Why else would you lay down with me and have two children? If there were no feelings involved, you would have left me alone after we had Carmelo."

"You really want to know why we ended up having two children? It's because I was fucking stupid and wanted to fuck. I didn't care who I was fucking. However, you just happened to be convenient pussy that I could hit raw, and it's just as simple as that."

I scoffed. "Nigga, please! You love me!"

"I'm done with this conversation…" He turned to walk away from me.

"Are you fucking serious?"

He spun around and looked me up and down like I meant nothing. "Go home, Kim. I'll handle everything from here. And leave Paige the fuck alone."

I smacked my lips. "I'm not leaving my kids! You must be out your mind. And fuck your bitch! I do what I want."

"Yo, what I say? Go home, Kim. I got it from here, and I think the kids should stay with me for a while until we get this shit figured out." He walked away, leaving me defeated.

This was one hell of a night.

Chapter Eighteen

DE'ARRA

"Hey, sissy, you okay?"
I found her in the bathroom, splashing her face with water.

"Yes, I'm fine. I think it's crazy how last night I felt completely done with Millz and was glad Tre came to my aid. Millz was the furthest thing from my mind today until I saw him in the hospital with that bitch. Then he had the nerve to say it was for a miscarriage, which meant that he did, in fact, get that bitch pregnant again while we were still together. It just really hurts because I was nothing but good to that man, and all he did was cause me trouble and blacken my eyes. I didn't deserve any of that, but it's cool. I'm good, at least for right now. I promise. What about you?" She grabbed a napkin to wipe her wet face.

I sighed. "Trust me, I feel you on that one hundred percent. You have every right to feel the way you do, especially after sticking things out with him, hoping he would become the man he used to be. I'm glad that you can see now that he isn't going to change and is going to continue doing the same dumb shit that he's been doing. Now, as far as my situation is concerned, I'm just really confused about how Izzy even knows Kim. And the fact that she even called him to be her 'shoulder to cry on' doesn't sit well with me. I don't know where we stand, but as of now in this moment, I don't think I want to continue anything with him. He's such a liar. It's just so much going on. I feel like my head is about to explode."

"I know. So, how about this? Let's just leave for a little. We can go find food and allow the guys some space. Sound good?"

My grumbling stomach sounded like a baby's gurgling noise, which caused us to both laugh. "Hell, yes. I'm down for that plan."

"My car is still at Assad's, so I'll order an Uber." Paige pulled out her phone as we exited the bathroom.

* * *

"Where are y'all coming from?" Assad quizzed as we came around the corner an hour and some change later, laughing and chatting about nothing in particular.

I felt a little better about my crazy ass situation, especially after having food in my belly. Assad was sitting next to a little boy, who I assumed was Trevin's.

"We caught an Uber to get something to eat."

"Oh, okay. You should have told me. My driver could have taken y'all."

"It's cool. We didn't want to be a bother."

"You could never bother me, mama, but I get it. I don't see any leftovers for me, though," he joked as I looked over my shoulder at my sister. I could tell he was just making small talk, but I could see the pain in his eyes, so I wanted to chat alone.

"Let me talk to him right quick," I said to Paige.

"Okay, girl. I'm going to go say goodbye to Tre. It's late, and I'm tired."

I nodded and sat next to Assad. I grabbed his hand and gave it a squeeze.

I gave him a small smile as he looked over at me. "How are you feeling?"

"I'm good. This is just... it's a lot to take in, but thank you."

He surprised me with his words. "For what?"

"Being here. I know it's a lot going on tonight with my grandmother passing, then you seeing ol' boy with another woman. This is just a lot, and I thank you for being here for hours with us... well, me."

"Let me tell you something. Just because we just met doesn't mean I can't be here for you and that you don't deserve to have someone in your corner supporting you. I'll stay here with you all night if I have to. I don't mind. Well... I mean... hospitals do make me a little uneasy because I always think about the bad memories from when my mom passed. But if you're okay with me leaving out for fresh air every once in a while, then I can stay."

"Thank you, but it's okay." He gave my hand a squeeze. "It's late, and my nephew should be in bed, but I know my brother didn't want him to go home with Kim tonight, so I'm going to take him home. I can't believe she had him sitting out here by himself with a stranger."

I shook my head. "I can. She doesn't seem to be the brightest."

"Yeah, I agree. But, uh... I already reached out to the funeral home in regard to picking up my grandmother's body, so we can really leave right now."

"Okay."

Assad stood up and pulled me up with him. As he pulled me into a hug, I wrapped my arms around his waist, and my body just melted into his. He then kissed my forehead.

"Let me holla at my brother, and I'll be right back. Then, we can go home and get your sister back to her car."

Home, huh? It has a little ring to it.

"I like the sound of that."

He kissed my forehead once more before picking up his nephew and leaving me in the lobby.

Chapter Nineteen

TREVIN

"Hey." I looked up to see Paige standing in the doorway of my daughter's hospital room.

The night I had was definitely one for the books. Our grandmother passed, and my baby could have died, all because her hoe ass mama was playing house with the next nigga and barely paying them any attention. She knew I didn't want anyone around my kids. The thought alone made my blood boil.

"What's up, mama?" I gave her a faint smile, and hers matched mine.

"I'm about to leave for the night. Are you good?"

I sighed, temporarily looking away from my baby and then back over at Paige. "Honestly, I'm as good as I'm going to be regarding the situation. They are going to discharge her in the morning. They said her vitals and everything looks good, but honestly, moving forward, I'm definitely going to look into getting full custody."

She nodded. "I don't have any children, but I completely understand why you feel this way. I say go for it. It may be a little hard with you being on the road a lot, but you definitely strike me as the type of person who will figure it out. I like that about you, and I'm really glad that baby girl is okay." She yawned, then quickly placed her hand over her mouth. "I'm so sorry. I'm beyond tired, and that was rude."

I chuckled. "You're good, mama. I also want to thank you for just being here tonight. I know you want to practically run for the hills after all the drama you've been going through since you met me, but the fact that you stayed and thugged it out for this long definitely says a lot. I appreciate you more than you know."

"Aww, you're so welcome."

Standing up, I pulled her in for a hug and placed a kiss on her cheek. "Sweet dreams."

"Thanks. The same to you."

We bid each other goodbye, and there was only a few moments of silence between me and my sleeping baby girl before my brother walked in, holding my son, who was also sleeping.

"Listen, bruh, I'm about to head home. Just pick him up in the morning, and when you're in a good headspace, we can discuss Grandma's funeral."

"Okay, and thank you."

"Anything for Uncle's babies. I'd die behind them, and you know that."

I burst out laughing, making sure not to be too loud. "Nigga, don't ever say 'Uncle's babies' again.

"Nigga, fuck you. I'll see you in the morning." My brother was a fool and always had been.

Just like that, my brother had come and gone, leaving me to think and shit.

I didn't know how I was going to raise two small children full-time while I was just getting started with my rap career, but I knew God would guide me every step of the way. My best bet was to stop worrying and let the chips fall where they may.

DE'ARRA

"Okay, lil' man is tucked in and still sound asleep."

Assad came and sat next to me on the couch as I picked up the remote.

"Did you want to try and watch a movie or a show? I'm sure it'll keep your mind off things."

He got comfortable, surprisingly scooting closer before placing his arm behind me on the couch. "I'm down with whatever you want to watch, mama. I'm not picky."

"You say that now, but if I put on a sappy romance movie, I don't wanna hear any complaints."

He laughed. "I said what I said. Put on what you like."

"Okay." I settled for the new season of *Love is Blind*. I was a sucker for the show but hadn't been able to watch the new season yet due to my refusal to pay Netflix's high ass pricing.

"What's this?"

"Oh, it's really good. It's about couples who pretty much fall in love through a wall without ever seeing each other. Then, they have to propose to someone, meet in person for the first time, live together, meet each other's friends and family, and all that good stuff. In the last episode, we see who actually decides to get married."

"Damn, that's tough. I don't think I'd be able to do that."

"Why is that? Do you feel like you have to be physically attracted to someone before committing?"

He shrugged. "Honestly, I'm a different kind of nigga. Yes, I would love for my lady to be eye candy and break niggas' necks when she walks in the room, but having a real, genuine connection with someone is fucking amazing. To meet someone who is your soulmate, a person who gets you, is there for you, your best friend, and all that shit trumps the physical. The reason I said I might not be able to do that is only because of the fact that I like physical touch. I love looking into your eyes, smelling your scent, watching you blush, how you eat, connecting while I'm deep in your shit, and all that. With getting to know someone through a wall, I won't get to see, feel, or smell none of that."

"Damn." I chuckled. "Now, I didn't expect that from you, but I agree one hundred percent. I love watching the show and seeing people fall in love in untraditional ways. However, I am definitely a traditional girl. I'd fail this experiment big time, and then the fact that it's like a group of about twenty men and women all dating and falling for possibly the same person is blowing me. I don't want any other hoes dating my man."

"Let me find out you're possessive."

"Of my man, I am." We were so into our conversation that the TV was watching us instead of the other way around.

"Could you see yourself being possessive over me?" I didn't know why, but his asking me that question made my heart flutter.

"Only time will tell."

"I could see myself falling in love with you."

Bitch, he's laying it on thick!

"Is that what you're looking for? Love? A partner? A wife?"

"To be honest, I'm not looking for anything at all right now, but I have a feeling that you and I will grow closer. You being here wasn't accidental, De'arra. It was fate."

Silence fell upon us. It was like time had stopped as our faces gravitated toward each other. He stared lovingly into my eyes, and the second his lips grazed mine, I just couldn't control myself. I placed my hand on the back of his head.

Our lips locked, and I moaned when he hopped up with our lips still connected and pushed me down gently onto the couch to where he was on top of me. His tongue slid into my mouth with ease, and before I knew it, we were making out without a care in the world, that is, until his dick started to brick up. As bad as I wanted to explore things with him, this wasn't the right timing. I placed my hand on his chest and slowly pushed him back.

"What's wrong?" he breathlessly asked, searching my eyes for the answer.

"I like you... I mean, I've been enjoying getting to know you so far, but I think we should slow things down a little. I don't want us to have sex just because we're caught up in the moment. I'm upset with my boyfriend or lack thereof, and you're grieving your grandmother, so I could see how we easily got into this position. If this is going to happen between the two of us, I want it to be done the right way. Unlike most girls that you may be used to, I'm not just an easy piece of ass."

"For one, I never viewed you as an easy piece of ass, so let's just get that straight. Second of all, I respect you, so if this is not something you want to do, I'm cool with that. We can finish watching this weird ass show with the people falling in love through a brick wall for all I care."

I couldn't help but laugh as we both adjusted ourselves and sat back upright on the couch. "Sir, shut up."

"I'm just saying, mama, I don't mind watching the show as long as I get to spend time with you."

I looked over at him. "You know, you're actually kind of sweet. I like that about you. You seem to be in touch with your feelings, and you aren't afraid to say what's on your mind. You really communicate well."

"See, that's what happens when you deal with a very grown and mature adult male. The nigga you call your man could never compare to me, even on my worst fucking day."

"See, I would agree with you, but that would just be wrong. Instead, I'll just press play on the show since it somehow got paused."

"It got paused because you were all over me. I'm fine as shit, so I see why you almost sucked my dick up through my pants."

I gasped, hitting him in the chest. "I did not. Shut up and watch the TV."

"Give me one more kiss, and I'll let you watch this shit in peace."

"Assad." I glared at him, trying hard not to blush. "Really?"

"Here, let me help you out, mama." He placed his hand under my chin and leaned in, kissing me ever so sweetly on the lips.

God, this man! I just can't!

After about three pecks, he pulled away, smirking as if he just knew he had me under his spell.

"That was three kisses, not one."

He chuckled. "Just watch the show, baby."

Izzy who?

Chapter Twenty

TREVIN

"Oh, shit. My bad."
I woke up to see the sun coming up. The little couch they had in my baby's room was comfortable as shit, so I wasn't surprised I'd slept through the night. I headed into the bathroom that was inside the room, and there was a whole naked woman in there for whatever reason.

I quickly turned to leave, but she stopped me, grabbing my arm.

"It's about time you woke up." She was beautiful, and her body was a work of art, but I was confused. Her titties sat perfectly, and her makeup was perfectly beaten like an egg or whatever the fuck women said when their makeup looked good.

As I looked her up and down, I noticed that her toes were done with a French manicure. Her pussy was shaved, and her nails were on point along with her lace front, where I couldn't even see the lace. Shawty was bad, no doubt.

"I'm sorry. Who are you?"

The caramel beauty giggled, making her titties bounce. "Your number one fan, silly. When my home girl, who shall not be named, called and told me that Tre Bang was up in the hospital, I had to come and see for myself. Hell... it's a bunch of paparazzi outside, so somebody obviously tipped them off, but I found a way to slide right past them."

Stepping closer into my personal space, she pressed her titties against my chest and wrapped her arms around my shoulders, but I slowly shook them off me.

"Uh... nah. I'm good, mama. I'll step out so you can get dressed."

I opened the door and bumped directly into Paige.

Fuck

"Umm..." Paige dramatically poked her head inside the bathroom, causing ol' girl to cover herself with her hands.

Paige held a McDonald's breakfast bag and a cup of coffee. "Well damn, and good morning to y'all. I came to check on you and make sure that you at least ate something. If I knew you had company up here, I would've brought extra food and coffee," she joked as I fully stepped out of the bathroom and let the door close behind me.

"Don't do that."

"Do what? Your child is laid up in a hospital bed, and you are in the bathroom of her hospital room trying to get pussy." She paused to gather her thoughts as I peered down at her. "You know what? You're not my man, so here's your food... here's your coffee... I'm out."

After handing me the food and coffee, she tried to walk out, but I stopped her. "Paige! I swear on everything I love that I don't even know her. I woke up, went into the bathroom to take a piss, and this bitch was naked."

Glaring at me, she said, "It's cool. Like I said, I just came to make sure you were good." Looking me up and down, she also said, "Looks like you're just fine to me."

"Listen... hold up."

A few moments later, the woman walked out of the bathroom fully dressed. Paige scoffed as the woman slid me a piece of paper.

"Call me when you're ready for a real woman."

"Bitch!" Paige lunged at ol girl, but I hemmed her lil' ass up.

To Be Continued...